MW01406248

GHOULISH BOOKS
San Antonio Texas
www.GhoulishTales.com

Ghoulish Tales—Issue #2
Copyright © Ghoulish Books 2024
(Individual stories copyright by their respective authors)
All Rights Reserved

ISBN: 978-1-943720-92-7

The stories included in this publication are works of fiction. Names, characters, places and incidents are products of the authors' imaginations or are used fictitiously. Any resemblance to actual events or locales or persons living or dead is entirely coincidental.

Without limiting the rights under copyright reserved above, no part of this publication may be reproduced, stored in or introduced into a retrieval system, or transmitted, in any form, or by any means (electronic, mechanical, photocopying, recording, or otherwise), without the prior written permission of both the copyright owner and the above publisher of this book.

PUBLISHERS:
Max Booth III & Lori Michelle Booth
EDITOR GHOUL: Max Booth III
LAYOUT DESIGN GHOUL: Lori Michelle Booth
ART GHOUL: Betty Rocksteady
SLUSH ASSISTANT GHOUL: Mindy Rose

CONNECT WITH US

Patreon:
www.patreon.com/ghoulishbooks

Website:
www.Ghoulish.rip

Facebook:
www.facebook.com/GhoulishMagazine

Twitter:
@GhoulishTales

Instagram:
@GhoulishBookstore

Newsletter:
www.PMMPNews.com

Linktree:
www.linktr.ee/ghoulishbooks

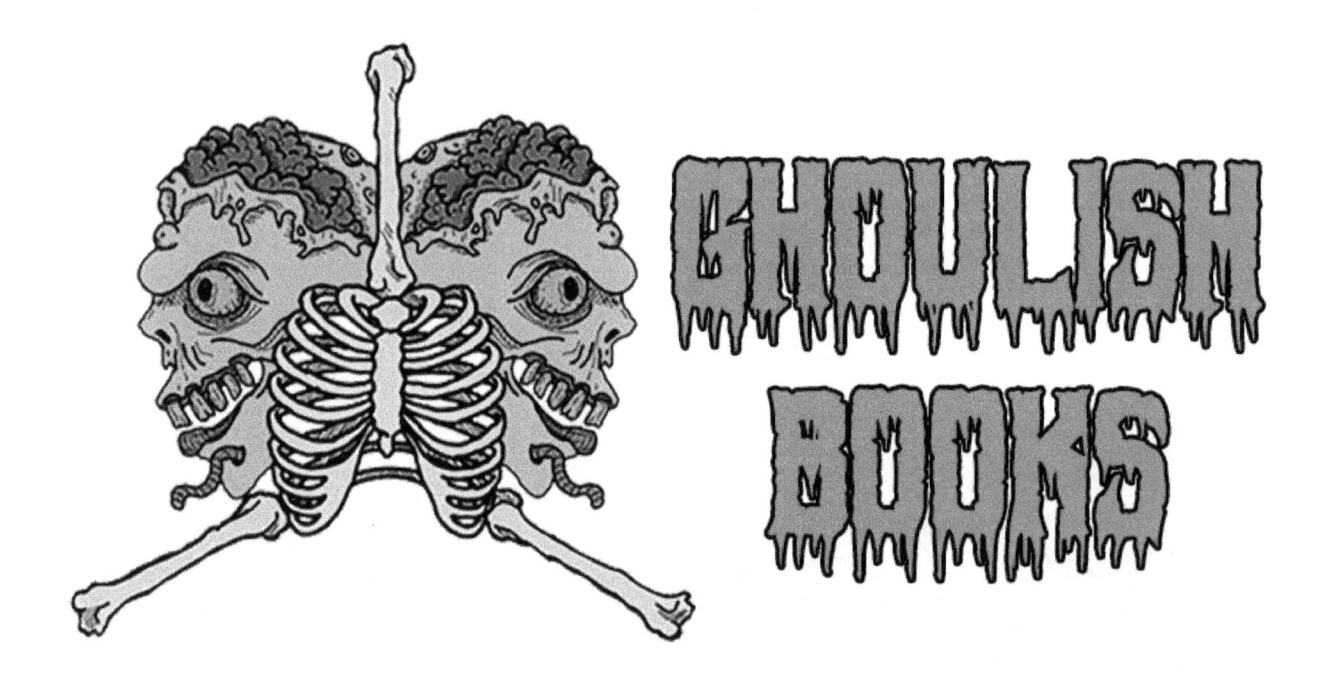

A THANK YOU TO OUR 2023 KICKSTARTER SUPPORTERS

A. C. Knight, A. J. Conway, Ada Ostrokol, Adrian, Adrian Shotbolt, Agatha A., AingealWroth, aj, Alejandro Figueroa, Alex Ebenstein, Alex Rodriguez-Acevedo, Alexander (Beast) Luthy, Alvaro Rodriguez, Amanda Hard, Amy Gijsbers van Wijk, Amylou Ahava, Andi, Andrew Hilbert, Andrew Kozma, Andrew Shaffer, Andy Martino, Angel Leal, Angel Luis Colon, Anna Dodson, Anna M Valles, Anthony Bowman from The Frankencast, Ariana Limone-Ryan, Audry Olmsted, Austin Hofeman, Austin Wilson, Autumn Pike, Ava Dickerson, Bea Goode, Becca Futrell, Becky Robison, beedeebrave@gmail.com, Benoît Lelièvre, Betsy Nicchetta, Betty Rocksteady, Beverly Bambury, Bill, Bill Kohn, Bill Sizemore, Bill T, Bob DeRosa, Bob Pastorella, Bobby H., Brad Sanders, Brandon & Candice Held, Brandon Santana, Brent Jones, Brian Huff, Brian King, Brian M, Brooke Gessner, Brooke Kennelley, Buffalo Billie, C Billow, C. D. Kester, C.R. Langille, Cai Murphy Ritenour, Campbell R., Caroline, Caroline Coriell, Carter, Cemetery Gates, Charles M., Charlie Wellman, Charlotte Platt, Chess Ruby, Chris Baumgartner, Chris Williams, Christian D Leaf, Christina Morris, Claire, Clay and Meade Byers, Clay McLeod Chapman, Collin Martino, Corey Doerr, Craig Hackl, Cynthia Petersen, Dai Baddley, Dakota Reinhart, Damia Torhagen, Dan and Summer Smith, Dan Scamell, Daniel Moore Hinton, Daniel Vlasaty, Daniel, Trista, and Eleanor Robichaud, Danielle Stachnik, Darcie Nadel, Dave Urban, David Cross, David Demchuk, David Hoffman, David K., David Myers, David Raposa, David Worn, Dawn Colclasure, Daxh A., Dead Fishie, Dennis Tafoya, Denver Grenell, Destiny Andrews, Diversity in Horror, Don Lee, dwbrid80@gmail.com, Dylan B, E. M. Roy, Ed Grady, Elizabeth Guilt, Elizabeth R McClellan (popelizbet), Em, Emily Walter, Emma J. Gibbon, Emmy Teague, Eric K, Eric Raglin, Erica H. Walsh, Erica Robyn, Erik Smith, Ethan Hutchinson, Eve Harms, Francesca Ripley, Franco Guarino, Frederick Rossero, Full Throttle Sound, Gage Gaiss, gallenmartin@gmail.com, Gardner Linn, Gareth Jones, Gary N. Parenteau, Gavin P, Geoff Emberlyn, Giusy Rippa, Grant Longstaff, Hadley S., Hailey Claire Hull, Hailey Piper, Haley H., Hana Correa, Hannah Janda, Holly Benavente, House of Blood, How is that Night?, Ian Chant, Ifeanyi Esimai, Illeana, izsch2, J Manchester, J.M. Brandt, Jacen Leonard, Jakii Culver, James Fitzsimmons, James Wilson, Jamie J., Jarne Van Vooren, Jason McCoy, Jay Slayton-Joslin, Jeanine Long, Jeff Meyers, Jeffrey C., Jenny Underwood, Jeremiah Israel, Jerry Purdon, Jes Malitoris, Jesse Zurlino, Jessica McHugh, jhenrymckeen@yahoo.com, Joanne A., Jodee Stanley, Joe butler, John Alex Hebert, John Baltisberger, Jonathan Brown, Jonathan Gensler, Jonathan Knell, Jonathan L, Jonathon M. Smereka, Joseph Z., Josh & Karin Swope, Josh Buyarski, Joshua Cooper, Justin Lewis, Justin Lutz, K Petrin, Kalyn W, Katlina Sommerberg, Kayli Scholz, Kelly Hoolihan, Kenny Endlich, Kevin H., Kevin Lemke, Kevin Thomas, Kevin Wadlow, Kirsten Murchison, Kris Breighner, Kristina Meschi, Kye, Kyle J Shepherd, L.P. Hernandez, Laura Goostree, Laurel Hightower, Lauren Bolger, Lauren Carter, Lauren Roberts, LC von Hessen, Leftie Aubé, Leslie Twitchell, Linda and Larry Winzenread, Lionel Ray Green, Lisa Westenbarger, Logan Moore, Lottie Biscotti, LT Williams, Lunar Violet, LuPa, M Baker, M. Allen, M.Bouckaert, Madeleine Koestner, Mae Murray, Maggie L. Omaña, Magnus Lima, Malachi Abell, Mandy Bublitz, Margaret A., Mari B, Maryanne Chappell, Mason Hawthorne, Matt Brandenburg!!, Matt Henshaw, Matt Ramsey, Matt Stepan, Matthew Walker, Max B., Megan Kiekel Anderson, Megan Mccullum, Mel Layos, Melissa Cox, Mia Tylia, Michael A. Cook, Michael Cieslak, Michael G. O'Connell, Michael Louis Dixon, Michael Paul Gonzalez, Michael R., Michelle Glatt, Michelle Quaynor, Miguel Myers ATx, Mike McCrary, MindyLeeReads, morda sam, MortalTraveler, Najwa Red, Nate Bondurant, Nic Knack, Nick Kolakowski, Nicolas, Nicole Sadenwater, Niko Thompson, Nikolas P. Robinson, Nisha Hollis, Norbert Böhm, Paige Holland, Pat Bevins, Pat S., Paul Buchholz, Paul Cardullo, Perry M, Polyeurythane, Preston F., Prince Eric Vickers, R. C. Hausen, Rain Corbyn, Ray Reigadas, ReArcangeli, Regino, Rena Mason, Reneé Hunter Vasquez, Renee Pickup, Res Bratton, Ria Hill, Riley R., River Hudgins, River Onei, RJ Joseph, Robbie Dorman, Robert Mikkelson, Roger Venable, Rose O., Ryan Booth, Ryan C., Ryan C. Bradley, S. Kay Nash, S. White, Sadie Cocteau, Sam Kurd, Sam Logan, Samantha Eaton, Sandra Ruttan & Brian Lindenmuth, Sara Corris, Sarah McGinley, Sarah P, Schatzi, Scott Adlerberg, Scott Hastings, Sean Ford, Sean Leonard, Sebastian Ernst, Sergey Kochergan, Seth, Shane Hawk, Shannon Bradner, Sharon Levy, Shelly Lyons, Sheri White, Shrader Thomas, Siobhan Dunlop, Siobhan Thomas, Sirrah Medeiros, Skip Zepeda, Sofia Ajram, Sophia Lebar, Sophie Newman, Stephanie Brantner, Steve Irwin, Steve Loiaconi, Steve Pattee, Steven Campbell, stevenroy@gmail.com, Stevie McJigglemeats, Suppi, Susan Jessen, Tai Black, Taliesin Neith, Tanya Semmons, Tav Jackson, Tenebrous Press, Teresa B. Ardrey, The ARC Party, The Blerd Newsletter, Theresa Derwin, Thomas Joyce, Thurston Howell VIII, Tim Meyer, Tobias Carroll, Todd Keisling, Tom Deady, Tore Nielsen, Trevor Olsen, Victor Adam Garcia, Victoria Nations, Warren Wagner, Webberly Rattenkraft, William Jones, Witchyjazzy, Yve Budden, Zach Low, and Zachary Locklin.

A SPECIAL THANK YOU TO OUR PATREON SUPPORTERS

A. H. Plotts, Adam Rains, Adrian Shotbolt, Amanda Niehaus-Hard, Antony Klancar, Betty Rocksteady, Bob, Bob Pottle, Brad Sanders, Brett Reistroffer, Chazzaroo, Chris Baumgartner, Christopher Barr, Claudia J Parker, Clay Waters, Cullen Wade, Daniel Scamell, Dave, David Demchuk, David Perlmutter, DeerNoises Emma Williamson, Erin Murphy-Jay, Eve Harms, Fox Morphis, gengar, George Daniel Lea, Gina Piantoni, Grant Longstaff, Gregory A. Martin, Ian Muller, Jack Smiles, James (Tony) Evans, Jampersand, Jason Kawa, Jennifer McCarthy, Jesse Rohrer, Jessica Leonard, Jessica McHugh, Joe Z, John Foster, Jose Triana, Julie Cyburt, Kevin Lovecraft, Lisa, Matthew Booth, Matthew Brandenburg, Matthew Henshaw, Michael Kazepis, Miguel Myers, Mistina Picciano, Myrmidon, Nat Weaver, Neil, Night Worms, Nikolas P. Robinson, Rachel Cassidy, Rebecca, regrettable_conscience, Richard Staving, Rob Gibbs, Roger Venable, Ryan Jenkins, Sammynona, Samuel Peirce, Scott Adlerberg, Scotty Nerdrage, Shelby MacLeod, Sheri White, Steve Ringman, Stewie, This Is Horror, Thomas Joyce, Todd Keisling, Traci Kenworth, Webberly Rattenkraft, Will Griskevich, and William Hull.

DID YOU KNOW GHOULISH BOOKS NOW HAS A PHYSICAL RETAIL STORE?

The rumors are true! We have officially opened our own horror-themed bookstore in the Greater San Antonio Area. In addition to books, we also host weekly movie nights, writing clubs, book clubs, and much more!

Come on down to Ghoulish Books at
9330 Corporate Drive, Suite #702,
Selma, TX 78154
for all your spooky needs.

GHOULISH TALES

Issue #2

Fiction

Skulls 9
    by Jen Conley

What It Takes to Swallow a Dog..13
    by Stephanie M. Wytovich

The Halloween Horror Show..19
    by Lena Ng

Print or Die..24
    by Justin Lutz

A Certain Level of Discretion 34
    by Jess Hagemann

The One With the Gas Station 37
    by Shannon Riley

Hair Problems 46
    by Danger Slater

Lucy West is Not a Stage Name 56
    by Jennifer Elise Wang

The Skin of Reema Lal 60
    by Saswati Chatterjee

Jude Doe..64
    by perfect kiss strickoll

Non-Fiction

Goop by Goop: Blobiversary Edition 31
    by Lor Gislason

The Act-One Dog: Animals & Horror...53
    by E. F. Schraeder

BE A GHOUL ON THE GHOULISH DISCORD

Join nearly 1,000 other ghouls on the Ghoulish discord! Discussions range anywhere from the best horror books currently being published to whether or not it's appropriate to make love while wearing socks.

There's even a book club!

ABSOLUTELY NO CATFISHING ALLOWED (WE'RE LOOKING AT YOU, PRESTON).

https://discord.gg/cbtk7EdhSt

CELEBRATING STIGMAS IN TIMES OF ATROCITY

We live in a world of horror. Some is good horror. A lot of it is bad horror. Most of it is bad horror.

We are suffocated by the atrocities of this universe on a daily basis. Sometimes it feels like there is no escape, and that is because there *isn't* an escape.

We are trapped.

The only option we have is to momentarily flee into other horrors—the good horrors. Books, movies, television—these are the good horrors. These can be the fun horrors.

This magazine is meant to be a fun horror. Something that makes you excited about a genre so often criticized by the general population. A celebrated stigma. A reminder of why you love reading. Because I lied a moment ago, when I said there is no escape. Stories are an escape. This has been true since the beginning of time. When the sun goes down, and the darkness consumes us all, we will still have stories.

Stories are many things. They are distractions, yes, but they are also how we understand the world. Stories help us make sense of the unexplainable. They're therapy sofas. They're Rorschach tests. Every story is a puzzle, and the finished result is different every time you look at it. Stories are also entertainment, which is critical in times of vileness. Stories are medicine with multiple purposes and we must never take them for granted. When we have nothing else, we will still have stories, and I think that is the most beautiful truth in the world.

These things are easy to ignore. Spend enough time doomscrolling and you will forget how to experience joy. You will forget how to function.

I am not claiming *Ghoulish Tales* is anything special other than a good goddamn time. I would never want it to be anything more.

This is issue two of our little magazine. It's several months behind schedule and frighteningly over budget, but that's okay. It's only a magazine. These are only stories. Stories I happen to have fallen in love with—and stories I hope you fall in love with, too.

Some of these writers I was already familiar with, but several of them I'd never heard of until coming upon their submissions in the slush pile. Discovering new writers and having the honor of publishing their very first stories, giving them that debut publication spot, it's one of the primary joys I have left when it comes to working in publishing. It's not an easy business. We will probably never make back what we spent on this issue, or any other issue, past or future. Each issue costs thousands of dollars that we have to frantically scrape together to pull off. This is not a brag, but a reality. So I just want to thank you, dear ghoul, for giving *Ghoulish Tales* a chance. For buying a copy and reading these wonderful authors. For—hopefully—telling your friends about the publication, and recommending it to every single human being you pass on the street going forward (or backward).

I hope, if anything, this issue introduces you to your next favorite writer.

And, if I could hope one more thing, it would be that these horror stories cure whatever ails you. They probably won't—not completely, anyway—but I can still hope. And so can you.

—Max Booth III
February 3, 2024

Subscribe to
𝔗𝔥𝔢 𝔊𝔥𝔬𝔲𝔩𝔦𝔰𝔥 𝔗𝔦𝔪𝔢𝔰

Keep yourself updated with everything going on in the world of GHOULISH by subscribing to our newsletter, The Ghoulish Times!

Essays, interviews, and even occasional fiction! Plus, photos of our cute dogs.

Everybody in your neighborhood is already subscribed.

WHY AREN'T YOU?

https://buttondown.email/ghoulish

SKULLS

Jen Conley

THE JANUARY AFTERNOON was cold and the boy, about eleven, stood in the mushy sand, the water of the bay's cove lapping quietly near his feet, the sun sinking in the sky. He held a skull in his hand. It was a bird's skull, small, grayish white, and with a long point—a crow or more likely, a seagull's head. It must've been a large seagull because the skull wasn't tiny enough to be anything else. This was the third skull he'd found in the past year, the first two were smaller—a squirrel's head and the skull of a dead cat. His mother wouldn't let him keep the skulls because she said they smelled and they didn't have a garage anymore since they moved to the townhome.

They had been walking through the woods and the marshes, along a nature trail, his mom, who was always tired, his sister, who was fourteen and angry, and himself. He could hear them talking, his sister arguing her case about why she should get her phone back, but his mom was standing firm. They were on the other side of the cove, having taken the trail around it, over the little bridge, to the other side. He couldn't see them across the water, which was covered with a delicate film of ice, but he could hear their echoes, his sister's voice rising up and down, fighting fiercely for her rights. Then he heard his mother shout, "I've had enough!" and all went quiet. At one point, he caught a glimpse through the trees of his mom's red jacket. They were going to walk to the end of the nature trail, take photos of the bay, then turn around and collect him. That was the plan.

The boy, whose name was Cole, took the skull back to the green metal bench near a patch of scraggly trees, tall reeds, and sticker bushes. In the summer, the bay and the cove would be filled with white boats, music, screaming, and American flags. But it was winter now, and the only evidence of the boat parties were the rusted beer cans caught in the brush, carried into the marsh by high tides and storms.

He turned the skull over. He wanted to take it home, bring it to school to show his friend, but decided that would be a bad idea. Liam Clark was on his bus and often grabbed Cole's backpack and looked in it. Liam lived in his complex, in section five, and always had a group of kids around him. Cole's sister called Liam an "annoying shit," and his mother said that Liam's home life was "unfortunate" which made him a bully. Liam lived with his mom and his older brother who had "issues" and his mother's boyfriend who was very large and lurked around like he was about to murder someone—that's what Cole's sister said.

Cole leaned back against the cold metal bench. A hawk circled above in the pink winter sky, dusk creeping in.

He heard the crack of the leaves.

And then there was an old man, holding a walking stick, wearing grimy clothes and torn gloves. His cheeks were sunken in, and his eyes were light blue. He nodded to Cole and sat next to him on the bench.

"That a bird's skull?" the man asked.

Cole nodded and peered across the cove in search of his mother's red jacket, but saw nothing.

"Give it here," the man said, and Cole, too nervous to say no, passed over the skull like he always passed over his backpack to Liam. Sometimes Cole wished that Liam was dead.

"Mmm," the man said, turning the skull over. Through the ripped gloves, Cole could see that the man's hands were big, with fingernails that were yellow and longish.

"Here," the man said, returning the skull. "You out here alone?"

The man unsettled Cole, and when he was unsettled, he lied. "My mom and my sister are over there." He pointed across the cove with its fragile ice. "And my dad is just back there." He pointed back toward the nature trail. "He'll be here any minute."

"Mmm," the man said.

The boy took a breath and tried not to think of what Liam had told him a month ago—that a serial killer lived out here. The killer didn't kill anymore, but he used to, mostly men but sometimes boys. Liam said he did weird things to them and then ate them. But the serial killer was too old now and couldn't kill like he used to. Society made him live out in the woods near the water because the police hoped he would drown in a storm, hoped a high tide would take him away, since they never got any evidence of his murders. Liam said the killer threw the bodies in the bay so the fish and crabs and boat motors could get to the dead boys and men before the Coast Guard could. When Cole told his sister this story, she said that Liam was a "stupid annoying shit" because there was no way they would keep a suspected serial killer out in the woods hoping for the tide to take him away.

"It's getting dark," the man said. He had a gravelly voice, and he stared at the boy with his intense blue eyes. "Very dark."

Cole shifted, holding his skull tightly, trying to find the courage to get up and run toward the nature trail. Yet he was afraid, afraid the man would grab him, do something bad. Recently, on a Friday night, Cole woke up in the middle of the night and got up. His mother's bedroom door was open, but his mother wasn't there. His sister's door was open, but she wasn't there. He went downstairs and found them both asleep on the sectional couch, each covered with a glossy gray blanket from Costco, Netflix playing on the TV.

When he turned to the screen, he saw a man with glasses holding a human head covered in plastic. Cole stood still, watching as the man examined the head until he put it in a wooden box. At that moment, his mother woke up, and then his sister opened her eyes, and his mother grabbed the remote and turned the TV off. "You shouldn't be watching it," she said and ushered him upstairs. "What was that?" he asked, but she said it was nothing. The next night, he saw them watching the Netflix show again, and his sister told him to go upstairs, that he was too young for it.

"I have skulls," the old man said. "I have real skulls, not bird skulls."

"Human?" Cole whispered.

"Mmm." The man nodded. "I used to find people, and I'd invite them to my house, and then I'd put something in their drink to make them sleep. Then I'd slit their throats." The man drew his grimy finger across his neck. "People think I buried them or put them on my boat and tossed them in the bay for the fish to eat. But I'd cut the bodies up. Toss an arm right in this water. A leg. Sometimes I'd take out the heart and watch the vultures and seagulls pick at it. But I always kept the heads." The old man grinned, his teeth as yellow and long as his fingernails. "I got a bunch."

Cole said nothing.

"I'd like to invite you to see my collection. You can bring your skull and put it next to my skulls."

The boy turned away and looked across the water with a film of ice, willing his mother and sister to return.

"It's getting dark," the man said. "My house is warm."

Just then, in the dimming light of the sky, he heard his sister's voice, loud and frustrated, and there, he saw his mother's red jacket. He stood up and called to them. "Hurry!" he shouted.

"That your mom and sister?" the old man said.

"Yes."

"But no dad, huh?"

"He's around."

"No, he ain't. I didn't see no man with you. I was watching."

Cole looked at the man who stood and winked. "I'm still here. I bet you could bring me a friend. I bet you're a lot like me."

"I gotta go." The boy ran toward the nature

trail, running and running, gripping his bird skull, until he met his mother and sister at the small bridge.

"You okay?" his mom asked.

He was going to tell them about the man but decided not to. He decided he would tell Liam. Tell him that he met the serial killer. Tell him he had all the skulls of all his victims. Liam would say he was lying, but Cole would dare him to go back into the woods. Alone. Dare him in front of Liam's friends. And Liam would say, "Then show me yourself."

And Cole would.

RAINBOW FILTH IS A WEIRDO HORROR NOVELLA ABOUT A SMALL CULT THAT BELIEVES A RARE PSYCHEDELIC SUBSTANCE CAN PHYSICALLY TRANSPORT THEM TO ANOTHER UNIVERSE.

ORDER YOUR COPY NOW!
WWW.GHOULISH.RIP

Introducing Laurel Hightower's THE DAY OF THE DOOR...in which three grieving siblings confront their manipulative mother after learning of her participation in a popular paranormal television show designed to dramatize the most traumatic day of their childhood, pitched as THE HAUNTING OF HILL HOUSE meets A HEAD FULL OF GHOSTS...

PRE-ORDER YOUR COPY NOW!

WWW.GHOULISH.RIP

WHAT IT TAKES TO SWALLOW A DOG

Stephanie M. Wytovich

RACHEL LASIDIC STOOD outside the door of Terrance McKinley's room as she watched the man with a hundred lacerations eat the gauze that had been applied to his wounds. His jaw seemed to work overtime as strips of cotton slid down his throat, his eyes two full moons that dared her to move, to do anything that would warrant him to stop.

She cracked her knuckles once, twice, three times before swiping her badge and opening the door.

"Mr. McKinley," she started, the recoil of the badge making a zipping sound as it retracted against her pant leg. "You know I have to ask you to stop."

"But I'm starving," he said, his voice a slur that fell out of a large fish-like mouth surrounded by wet slender lips. "I told them. I told them I couldn't wait, that the voices wouldn't listen. I have to eat. I have to feed them."

He struggled with the bindings that held him tight against the sheets, his body a tense, rigid board.

Rachel walked over to the bed and tightened the leather restraints on his arms and legs. "I'm sorry, but you know the drill. It's for your own safety, Terrance."

"Terry," he said, correcting her with a smile.

The room smelled of sweat-stained linen and the metal frame of the hospital bed seemed to crowd Terrance's thin body. Rachel tried to get him switched to a bigger room when she was first assigned to his case, but the administration wouldn't budge because they were already short on space.

"Let's do something about those wrists then, okay?" she asked, her tone tired but assuring.

She put on a pair of latex gloves and reached for the salve. Comforted by her touch, Terrance relaxed as she rubbed the ointment on his wrists, the mixture of tea tree and peppermint filling the room.

Outside, a storm raged as the wind smacked the window with a heavy hand. Branches scratched at the brick foundation while the rain whispered stories to the patients inside, its empty howls matching their own.

Terrance hadn't been at the hospital long, but he showed up often, always in some disheveled state as the authorities dragged him in for one thing or another. They'd get called to a scene for petty theft, disturbing the peace, or public urination, and then find the man trying to scoop out his stomach with a pen knife or eat someone's cat from their back yard. One time, he'd tried to cut the loose skin hanging from his neck and was in the hospital recovering for months, the foul stench of him enough to cause nurses to run from his room, vomiting in hallways and corridors. The staff hated him, mostly because they feared him, but no one was ever brave enough to turn him away.

"You're quite beautiful, you know" Terrance said, as Rachel removed her gloves and threw them in the biohazard wastebasket.

"Stop it," Rachel said, unable to hide her blush. "That's inappropriate, not to mention a lie."

STEPHANIE M. WYTOVICH

He made a movement to hold up his hands, almost as if to say 'if you say so,' but the leather straps only allowed his arms to move an inch or so.

Rachel smiled as she logged her notes.

Regardless of the cruelty of his acts, she couldn't help but feel bad for him. Afterall, it wasn't like he did anything to deserve this hunger, and the will to survive with it had to be both strong and horrific. All those late-night shows where people berated him with taunts and challenges, forcing him to stuff his gullet full of wooden boxes and flints. To swallow nails and bags of oranges. Just imagining the demons that spoke to him at night made her cringe, but it was the people who encouraged him, who paid to watch him perform that really churned her stomach.

The clock read 5:30 a.m.

"Here," said Rachel as she reached into her pocket. "I brought you something."

She handed him an apple and his eyes opened wide at the sight of it.

Hunger unabated.

"Thank you," he said, ravenous as if he hadn't eaten in weeks.

She placed the apple to his mouth and let him take a bite, the juice of the fruit running down her wrist as he fed, an eager child. It didn't matter that Terrance had only eaten a full meal two hours ago, or that he ate quadruple the amount of food a normal human ate in one sitting. Every time he saw her, he begged for more.

"Can you come a little closer? It hurts to stretch my neck like this," he asked.

Rachel leaned in a bit further and let him finish his snack. None of the doctors could figure out what caused the hunger. Sure, they speculated about hyperthyroidism and polyphagia, even the possibility that it stemmed from a brain injury, a tumor in the amygdala or hypothalamus, but regardless of what test they ran, or what therapist he spoke to, the results were always the same: normal.

One time she heard a group of doctors arguing about his case while she was on a smoke break. They were taking bets on when he'd die, on who would get to cut him open, examine the rot and toil that no doubt swam inside. One of them said she wanted to autopsy his brain. Another said he planned to take the stomach and see how much he could sell it for.

Rachel sat down in the tattered gray chair next to Terrance's bed. The smell of his yellowed teeth slid underneath her nose. The sight of his distended stomach made her queasy.

"Do you remember when we first met," she asked, watching him as he swallowed the apple core whole.

Terrace shifted in his bed, the rub of the restraints causing his eyes to water.

"Of course," he said. "It was after I got attacked by that dog."

Attacked.

Like it was an accident.

"Do you remember why the dog attacked you, Terrance?"

He searched the room for a moment, almost like he couldn't quite remember, as if mentally climbing the death-stained walls of this ceiling might offer a piece of the story, a memory repressed.

Rachel scanned his face and counted the slits in his skin.

One, two, three, four, five.

Claw marks. An attempt to survive, to get away.

Terrance chuckled and a quick simper rolled across his face.

"Because it didn't want to die," he said. "Can't say I blame it."

A darkness wove through the circles under Terrance's eyes as Rachel searched his face for a look of remorse, regret. There was so much blood that night. It stained the sheets, his hands. She remembered washing the red out of his blonde hair, conditioning it twice to get the fur and the smell of fight off him.

"Why did you do it?" she asked. "How could you do it?

"I already told you, Rachel," Terrance said. "I was hungry."

***

After a 12-hour shift, Rachel keyed into her apartment, slipped off her shoes and collapsed—fully dressed—on her couch. Her one-bedroom apartment was smaller than her dormitory room in college, but she hadn't seen a cockroach or a millipede in the past week, so she took that as a sign that the universe was smiling favorably upon her.

Hard to believe I pay $1,750 for this shithole.

WHAT IT TAKES TO SWALLOW A DOG

In the corner of her living room, the TV she never turned off played reruns of shows she never had time to watch. The fruit basket hanging near her refrigerator held wizened plums and browned bananas. She thought about filling up the kettle, but didn't have the energy to decide on which tea she wanted.

She did, however, think about Terrance McKinley.

When the police brought him in last week, he was covered in cuts and bruises, his lips chapped and bloody. He had been working as a traveling performer going from freak show to circus, swallowing live eels and rats, bushels of apples and dozens of eggs. The doctors had tried a list of treatments, both conventional and unconventional from tobacco therapy to opioids, but nothing curbed his insatiable appetite. Last she heard, they were speculating about hypnosis, trying to cure the demons of the mind in order to reach the physical manifestation of the disease within.

Personally, she didn't believe in that type of witchcraft.

In her mind, people were the only kinds of devils that existed.

Terrance's words replayed in her head: *"I told them. I told them I couldn't wait, but they wouldn't listen. I have to eat. I'm starving."* A part of her wondered what it felt like to have to feed like that, to take and take and never give back, to be all-encompassing, never satisfied. It was hard to imagine this small, hundred-pound man was the embodiment of gluttony, a true devourer.

Even still, she couldn't shake this feeling of unease that had wrapped itself around her shoulders. No one had ever looked at her that way. There was this raw desperation in his face, a countenance that pled, begged her without words. When he ate the apple form her hands, it was like feeding an animal, encouraging something that would eat itself to death if given the chance.

The idea was sexual, deviant.

Powerful.

She closed her eyes and dreamt about orchards overrun by packs of rabid dogs, the imagined scars on her face and arms open and bleeding.

***

Rachel woke up forty minutes later to find five missed calls and three voicemails, all from the hospital. The TV was running a story about a missing child, the parents on screen begging for his safe return.

She turned up the volume and rubbed her eyes as the ever-growing circles underneath threatened to pull her back to sleep. She made a mental note to start wearing concealer, though she knew the effort would never make it to her beauty routine.

"The search continues for 14-month-old Kyle Foster, who went missing from the ICU at North Chamber Hospital three hours ago. Terrance McKinley, 22, has also been reported missing by the staff, and police urge anyone with information about the whereabouts of either of these patients to please come forward," said Lauren Yale, the station's top reporter.

The number for the country police ran below her microphone next to a flashing AMBER ALERT sign.

Jesus fucking Christ.

The phone only rang once before she heard Mabel's voice scratch at her ear.

"Thank you for calling North Chamber Hospital—"

"Mabel," Rachel said, cutting her off. "It's Lasidic." She readjusted her sweat-soaked t-shirt and cursed herself for falling asleep with her bra still on. "Put one of the officers on now."

Static filled the space.

She remembered Terrance telling her about the pain earlier, about how it sometimes spoke to him at night while it ripped through his stomach, whispering to him to fill it full, full of death, full of life. Sometimes, he said he could still hear the animals inside him, their muffled whimpers and moans trapped inside his lungs, their hearts beating alongside his.

A mental picture of him swallowing the wet bodies of a basket of eels turned her stomach. She pictured him licking his lips, the taste of saltwater and struggle on his tongue.

What have you done, Terrance? What have you done?

"This is Officer Perry," a gruff voice said.

A knock came at the door.

Rachel hung up the phone, her mind reeling, her mouth agape. She pulled her hair back into a messy bun, her hands shaking.

"Just a minute," she said. Rachel picked up a

STEPHANIE M. WYTOVICH

half-empty glass of water from her coffee table and gulped down a mouthful or two before opening the door to two cops. Their nametags read Officer S. Martin and Officer J. Canterfield.

"Can I help you?" she asked, her voice cracking both from torpor and fear.

"Miss Lasidic, I presume?" Officer Martin asked. "Can we come in?"

Rachel nodded and motioned toward the living room.

"How—how can I help you? Is everything okay? I just called the hospital."

"I'm afraid not, Miss Lasidic," Officer Martin said. "Can I call you Rachel?"

Again, she nodded.

"According to Mr. McKinley's charts, you visited him this morning at 5:30 a.m. and administered a salve to his wrists to help with the irritation. Is this true?"

"Yes," she said. "I've been helping treat Terrance since he was admitted earlier this week."

"Can you tell me if at any point in your visit with Mr. McKinley he seemed violent? Distressed?" the officer asked, the pull of his deep blue eyes scanning her face for ticks and tells. "Did he say anything that might have upset you or struck you as strange?"

A picture frame of a weeping tree towered behind her. It made her feel small.

"No, he seemed fine. I mean, as fine as someone with his condition can be," she said. "He's naturally a bit on edge, as you can imagine."

Officer Martin nodded and seemed to fold in on himself, his hulking frame diminished by whatever he was about to ask.

"Some of the nurses have mentioned that Mr. McKinley has taken a liking to you. That he trusts you," he said, stumbling across his words. "Did he ever mention the name Kyle Foster before?"

"Kyle Foster? No, not that I can remember," she said, her mouth dry, a desert.

"See, Kyle Foster is a 14-month-old child who went missing earlier this evening from the ICU nursery. We pulled the entry records and your card was the last one used," Officer Martin said.

"But that's impossible," Rachel said. "I don't work ICU and I've been home all evening."

"Do you have anyone who could corroborate that?" Officer Canterfield asked.

The mental image of Terrance eating the apple from her hand raced through her head. She'd been close enough to him that she could smell the vomit on his breath, and if she was close enough to see the discoloration of his teeth, it could have been possible that, restraints or not, he snatched her badge from her waistband.

"No, not that I know of," she said. "I mean, I didn't run into anyone when I came home tonight."

"Do you have the badge on you now by chance?" Officer Martin asked.

Rachel reached for the card at her waist, and when it wasn't there, she grabbed her purse off the floor and frantically searched through it, moving around wallets and calendars, lipstick and compacts, but it wasn't there.

"It's possible that I may have left it in my locker," she said.

Officer Martin nodded and motioned to his partner.

"Sure. Why don't the three of us go check that out," Officer Martin said.

Rachel stood up to follow them, but then hesitated. "Am I under arrest?"

"Should you be?" Officer Canterfield said, the spit from his accusatory tone landing on her forearm.

"No, I—"

"Then you should have nothing to worry about," Officer Canterfield said. "But while we're here, do you mind if we take a look at the rest of your place?"

Rachel gave a weak smile and stepped aside. After a few tense moments, she followed them out to their car despite knowing in her gut, that she'd never once left her badge in her locker.

***

The metal doors reflected the red and blue wails of the police siren. Rachel looked around the crowded lobby and saw the glaring eyes of the hospital staff from behind the receiving desk.

Sweat collected on her neck.

The normal pit of anxiety in her stomach burgeoned.

"Just keep walking," Officer Canterfield said as he led her down the hallway.

Patients stared at her through the small slots in the doors.

"Has anyone checked the kitchens? The stock rooms?" she asked.

WHAT IT TAKES TO SWALLOW A DOG

Officer Canterfield nodded. "Yeah, we figured that would be the first place McKinley would go, but no such luck. We even checked the dumpsters, too, figuring he'd get desperate, but nothing."

They walked into the locker room and Rachel spun her lock to the appropriate coordinates. She opened the door and frantically search the contents inside. There were some crackers and an apple on the upper shelf, an extra pair of socks and underwear stuffed inside a spare pair of jeans on the bottom, but no badge. Her energy drink was gone too, but she doubted the two were related.

"It's not here," she said.

"Didn't think it would be," Officer Canterfield said. "You ready to tell us where it is now?"

Rachel swallowed hard.

"I honestly don't know. I suppose it's possible that Terrance could have taken it when I was in his room earlier today, but I mean, he was restrained to the bed," she said.

Silence filled the space between them.

"What aren't you telling me," asked Rachel.

In the distance, a woman screamed against the explosive sound of two quick gunshots that reverberated off the walls.

Rachel hit the ground, her hands covering her head.

"Stay down," Officer Martin whispered. "Don't move."

A clanging echoed down the hallway against the pitter patter of anxious footsteps outside the door. The shadow of a man climbed her locker, its breath ragged, fast, almost like an animal.

Terrance slid into the room panting, his back to the wall. His shoes left bloody footprints on the tiled floor. His eyes were wild and angry against the fluorescent light. When he saw Rachel, he bared his teeth, red and dripping, and let out a guttural sound, one that half-caught in his throat.

Rachel reached out and began to push herself up.

"Terrance, easy. It's me. Rachel," she said. "It's fine. You're okay," she pleaded, her eyes locked with his, searching for some semblance of humanity.

He titled his head as if he were trying to place how he knew her, as if the man in front of her had never seen her before, never told her she was beautiful.

He took a step toward her.

"Get down," Officer Canterfield said through clenched teeth, but Rachel eased toward Terrance, trying to calm the beast within.

More screams filled the hallway.

Terrance lunged then, his mouth open in bite.

Rachel cowered as the image of hunger imprinted in her mind, her world spinning as Officer Martin pulled out us gun.

It was done before she could beg, and then the room went acrid, sour as Terrance's body slumped on the floor.

***

The ambulance waited as the EMTs lifted Terrance McKinley onto the stretcher. Still breathing, albeit badly wounded, he was covered in blood and shaking, a rabid monster in heat. The lacerations on his face and neck seemed to pulse as they strapped him down, the white sheets on the gurney now a multitude of blossoming red.

Rachel had never seen so much blood come out of one person.

His hands, both in splints, were broken at the wrists, and she'd learned that he'd rubbed them to the bone as he pulled and tore against the leather until he was free.

"He broke both of his thumbs," a voice said.

"There were teeth marks in the restraints," another followed up.

After the gunshots, all Rachel heard was screaming.

The police initially found Terrance in the morgue, his face buried in the stomachs of corpses while he guzzled their drained blood like a starved vampire. They tried to reason with him, but he'd lunged at them like a rabid dog, his lips in snarl.

Again, she heard his voice: *"I told them. I told them I couldn't wait."*

Officer Martin handed her a coffee and wrapped a blanket around her shoulders. They brought out the body of Kyle Foster next, his small body overshadowed by the black bag that held it.

"The child had been dead for some time before it started," she heard the coroner tell the cops. "He ripped the breathing tube from his body, and there are bruises on his arms from where he was grabbed. Both of the legs are missing, chewed off down to the bone, bite marks on the chest and face."

Live Spooky, Die Spooky.

One of the officers threw up in the flowerpot next to the door.

Rachel stared at her feet, the world around her spinning.

To her left, reporters interviewed the parents of Kyle Foster. The man held his trembling wife as mascara bled down her cheeks and mixed with snot and spittle, her body slouched against his, too heavy to hold up on her own.

Officer Martin stood next to her, his face a ghastly white.

"What will happen to him now?" Rachel asked.

"I don't know," Officer Martin said. "If he's lucky, he'll die in that ambulance."

A tear rolled down her cheek. "I'm so sorry. I'm just so, so sorry."

Officer Martin put his arm around her as she sobbed.

"I know," he said. "Come on. Let's get you out of here. You don't need to see this right now."

Rachel wiped her face and followed him into the car.

The windshield wipers pushed the rain away as blood filtered off the streets and into the sewers.

Somewhere close, Terrance McKinley was dying.

And inside the car, the growl of a hungry dog ripped through her stomach, its teeth bare, the taste of apples on her tongue.

POCKETKNIFE KITTY

BY SHANNON RILEY

COMING 2024 FROM GHOULISH BOOKS

WWW.GHOULISH.RIP

THE HALLOWEEN HORROR SHOW

Lena Ng

FOR ONE NIGHT ONLY, of course on Halloween. The Halloween Horror Show, not for the delicate of heart. After the kids have done their trick or treating, instead of settling in to watch a movie you've seen a hundred times already, come see a real, live, horror show.

Are you prone to fainting? Do you have a heart condition? What the hell, come anyway to view the sentient, dreadful monsters. Come see the horrors only humankind can inflict. Spend a dollar to examine all the grotesqueries in the Halloween Horror Show. On this night only, the night where the realms of the natural and the unnatural overlap, can you see true reality, in all its mind-bending glory, beneath the sanity curtain.

Thank you for your dollar, sir. Ma'am, wander anywhere you want. There are no areas of the show that are off-limits. Except for the area at the back of show. That is for the new acts not yet ready. Do not go there. Now, are you ready to begin?

ACT I: DO YOU BELIEVE IN MAGIC?

There weren't many people in the audience. I could see why. The white rabbit with big floppy ears reappeared under the magician's top hat. It wrinkled its cute pink nose. Boring. The magician then unhooked three joined rings. Then he produced a bouquet of flowers from thin air and gave it to a sequinned-clad assistant. Nothing new. No, not card tricks! Could this show get any worse?

The magician asked for a volunteer. A lady dressed in a black gown jumped up and ran to the stage. I bet she was a plant. The magician fastened her to a round wooden board, each wrist in an iron manacle. She bit down on the scarf around her mouth. The magician brought out a long, shiny sword, swung, and severed one arm at the shoulder. This was repeated with the other arm. We were doused in hot, gushing blood. The magician took a bow. The lady's arms, however, did not grow back. He was not a good magician.

ACT II: FUN HOUSE

We giggled as the floor wobbled beneath us. We tumbled through the rolling barrel and jumped through a room filled with rubber balls. A trapdoor opened beneath us and we slid down a narrow, curving slide. The mirrors stretched our bodies and our smiles until we looked like Cheshire cats bursting with gleeful secrets. I turned to Jenny to laugh at how ridiculous we looked. She didn't seem right. What happened to her face? The weight of her head caused her body to fall forward. She moved along the floor like a slug using her teeth to gain traction. On my belly, I followed her into the moist, dark hole in the ground. I swallowed the dirt like an earthworm.

ACT III: MONSTER FISH WITH DEAD EYES

The smell was what hit us first. I plugged my nose and choked down the bile rising in my throat. On the ground lay a giant, fetid fish, as big as a bus. Its eyes were large, shiny, and vacant. What could it have seen in the depths of the ocean? What secrets hid in its alien-fish brain? It had a curved antenna growing from the top of its head, like a slimy, fleshy lure. I heard a muffled screaming. Through the slime, its large body had a jellyfish translucency. We could see what the fish had eaten. Their bodies were pressed against sides of the stomach. Maybe they were sailors, lost at sea. Or maybe they were immigrants whose boats had capsized. Inside the gelatinous belly, the fish food had melted faces. Still alive, they were being digested. Though the fish was dead, acid dripped from all sides of the giant fish's stomach. No one cut them out. Someone said send them back to their own country. I couldn't handle the smell and moved on to the next exhibit.

ACT IV: THE GEEK

The man crawled from the corner of the cage. Three chickens pecked at the floor. They weren't exotic chickens or anything, just regular chickens. The man crawled, but the chickens were good at moving away. This went on for eons. I glanced at my watch to decide how long I would give it. He was still crawling, the chickens still pecking. I don't think the man had eaten in ages. His face was gaunt and his arms looked like sticks covered in skin. His beard was scraggly and his hair was uncombed. He crawled in a slow-motion desperation. The chickens remained out of reach. He put a hand through the bars, but no one gave him anything. Let him earn his keep, I thought. People shouldn't rely on handouts. What was more horrific: the sight of an enslaved starving man or the spectacle of him biting off a chicken's head? Either way, it wasn't entertaining.

ACT V: THE TATTOOED MAN

The muscular man was dressed only in tattoos. From the bottom of his feet, which were coloured in green scales like a lizard, to the black of his ink-filled eyes. Even his bald head was covered in them—a ship, an anchor, a skull wrapped in roses. Gothic lettering trailed down the helix of his ears. When he stuck out his tongue, delicately-drawn seagulls flew along the red, bumpy sky. His body was a picture book, the story of his life.

He had tattoos of himself inked on his back. I knew it was him from the posture of his body. When I stared long enough, I thought I could pick up a thread of narrative. What did it mean: the mermaid, the tears, the knife buried in an altar? One tattoo was that of a fat, red heart, split down the middle. In one depiction, he wrestled with a horned devil. In another, he shook its talon with one hand while reaching into his chest with another. What did he give it? And in exchange for what?

In another scene, he was surrounded by the audience, displaying his body in all its inked finery. I recognized some of the audience members. One of them was me.

My face looked back at me from a small patch of skin. My expression was a mask of terror. What was embracing me in the tattoo? What was that monstrous shape, the coiled stingers, the tangle of clammy bodies? Was it the same thing as the mucous-covered limb now wrapped around my shoulders?

ACT VI: RESURRECTION

The man with the top hat asked for a volunteer. No one put up a hand so he pointed to an elderly man in the front row. The ringmaster whispered to the elderly man who nodded. He took off all his clothes. For modesty, the ringmaster gave the old man his top hat. One man wielded the mallet while another held steady the nails. After the old man had stopped moving, they took the body down from the cross. They laid him on the altar. He looked dead. Five congregants dressed in white dropped to their knees and began chanting. The body jerked and twitched beneath the shroud. He sat up and the cloth fell away. He raised his hands to show the holes. We all clapped although we disagreed with his teachings. The louder we clapped, the more we disagreed. He stretched a long arm and grabbed one of the supplicants by the throat. He bit the supplicant's neck. Colour returned to his face as he drank. Soon he no longer looked old.

ACT VII: TRICK OR TREAT

The bear was handing out candy. It wore a tiny red hat, tied with string beneath its jaws, and a

THE HALLOWEEN HORROR SHOW

crooked, red, glittery bowtie. It was dressed as a hurdy-gurdy monkey. An accordion, used as a prop, was left on the floor at its feet.

We lined up in a single row. When you got to the front of the line, the bear asked, "Trick or treat?"

The lady in front of me said treat.

It stuck a paw into the orange plastic jack-o'-lantern, and handed her a full-sized candy bar. We were getting our money's worth.

When I got to the front of the line, the bear asked, "Trick or treat?"

I also said treat. It reached into the jack-o'-lantern and handed me a caramel popcorn ball wrapped in tinfoil. I would've preferred a candy bar. Popcorn gets stuck in my teeth.

When the snot-nosed punk behind me was asked 'trick or treat?,' he said 'trick' because of course he would. The bear opened its jaws and bit off the kid's head. The headless body flailed around, his hands patting the ragged-edged stump, his legs tripping over themselves. The bear crunched on the skull with the ease of breaking an eggshell. It swallowed with great relish and rubbed its grumbly belly.

"That was a mean trick," I said.

The bear shrugged its shoulders. "It was a treat for me," it said.

ACT VIII: THE PUMPKIN PATCH

Silvery moonlight illuminated the fields. We ambled through the pumpkin patch where the gourds slept like slumbering giants. We picked up the machetes and hacked at the thick green vines, despite the illustrated warning signs and big, red letters. We were adults and could make our own decisions. We believed in freedom. We knew our rights. The pumpkins awoke and began dancing, albeit in a clumsy, hulking manner. Laughing, my college friend Ben and I began imitating them. They did not take kindly to this. Pumpkins must not have a sense of humour. They began barking. They began snarling. They were released from their green vine chains and now were free to hunt. One of them tried to squash me like a melon. They were, however, out of shape and had little gratitude for what we had done for them. We taunted them and kicked up our heels as we ran.

ACT IX: CORNFIELD MAZE

The corn stalks rustled in the October breeze. We wandered for hours. Every row looked like every other row, and there seemed to be an infinite number of them. I determined we were in purgatory. I tried to repent. I didn't do a good job, judging from the time we spent wandering, lost. In the middle of the maze there lived a monster. It hid under the ground. When we walked into the centre, it sprang from its trap. It grabbed my friend Ben with a clasp of hairy arms. It dragged him into its lair. Ben must not have repented while he still had the chance. I heard the crunch and snap of bones. Soon he stopped screaming.

ACT X: HAUNTED HOUSE

We were allowed in only one at a time. I crept forward, touching the walls with my hands. During one section, I had to crawl through a wet tunnel. I stepped into a familiar house, dark except for a snowy screen on the curved glass of a tube television. Once in a while, a cartoon dog would appear and rap on the glass. It seemed angry it was trapped inside such an old TV. I walked up the stairs. The floorboards creaked. A fly buzzed in a corner. A shadow loomed then disappeared. It stopped at the door to my bedroom, but didn't go in. The house smelled like the windows had not been open for months. A doll waved a thread-bare arm while hung upside-down on the ceiling. Voices whispered *put that back* and *you'll hurt yourself* and *go hide in the closet*.

In one room, mold grew in a lattice pattern on the walls. It pulsed like tiny arteries. A woman laid on a bed. Pill bottles crowded for space on the side table. Her hair covered her face. "I won't be getting better," she said.

"Rest now, Mom," I replied.

LAST ACT: THE END IS NIGH

In this last show, for your safety, you will be tied to your seats. The show has been said to be a little extreme. No need to stampede for the doors. There is no escape. It's too late for that anyway.

Do not be afraid. It will come in a form you may

not understand. That doesn't mean it acts in malice. It wants to understand. It wants to experiment. Brace yourself. It will only hurt for a minute.

Your arms and legs will bend in ways they have not bent before. Your head will turn around. Your spine may snap, but don't worry, it will mend. Look to the left. Look to the right. I hope you like the people sitting beside you. You will merge into one.

Awake in a daze. Awake in a sweat behind the iron bars in the off-limits area at the back of the exhibit. Mealtimes are at eight and six. Paw at the ground. Drool a little. Give 'em a sight never before seen. People will spend a hard-earned dollar to see you and all the other grotesqueries in the Halloween Horror Show.

BURY YOUR GAYS

A manifestation of ecstasy, heartache, horror and suffering rendered in feverish lyrical prose. Inside are sixteen new stories by some of the genre's most visionary queer writers. Young lovers find themselves deliriously lost in an expanding garden labyrinth. The porter of a sentient hotel is haunted within a liminal time loop. A soldier and his abusive commanding officer escape a war in the trenches but discover themselves in an even greater nightmare. Parasites chase each other across time-space in hungry desperation to never be apart. A graduate student with violent tendencies falls into step with a seemingly walking corpse. Featuring stories from Cassandra Khaw, Joe Koch, Gretchen Felker-Martin, Robbie Banfitch, August Clarke, Son M., Jonathan Louis Duckworth, M.V. Pine, Ed Kurtz, LC Von Hessen, Matteo L. Cerilli, November Rush, Meredith Rose, Charlene Adhiambo, Violet, and Thomas Kearnes.

PREORDER NOW!
WWW.GHOULISH.RIP

PRINT OR DIE

Justin Lutz

GATHERED AROUND THE PRESS, the three of them clutch travel mugs full of coffee and stare.

"I have no idea how this could have fucking happened," Kip says.

"You printed this sample before you left yesterday, right?" Sherry asks. She sips her coffee and shudders, something about the vandalism getting to her.

"Whoever did it," Cole says, sipping loudly, "they're not wrong." He laughs and the others cringe. Among the three of them Cole is the black sheep, the eccentric screen printer alone in the corner, bluetooth speaker bursting with tinny, crackling music that the others can rarely discern. Usually quiet, once in a while his facade crumbles and his true opinions bubble to the surface, anarchistic rants that make the other two simply nod and turn away.

"C'mon, man," Kip says, "you didn't do this?"

"Nope," Cole says. He turns and fires up the heating element on his conveyor dryer. "Almost wish I did, I was definitely thinking it."

On Kip's press is a sample for a police fundraiser that he set up and registered the day before. Splashed across the test print in giant, neon orange is the word *pigs*.

Kip prints all of the police-related jobs. Cole refuses on the basis of religious freedom, claims his religion is Anti-Fascist.

"Well shit, let's get this out of here before Steve sees it," Sherry says. Normally reserved, her face is flushed and her hands shake. She pulls the vandalized shirt from the press and balls it up, tosses it into the trash can. "Approved, Kip," she says. "Send it."

Cole rubs his phone and his shitty speaker comes to life, barely covers the sound of the dryers, the low squeak and clack of the turning presses. He's never been yelled at for his music, but keeps it low enough to play the game, knows the score. "Yo, Kip," he shouts from his side of the room, "this band is called MDC, you know what that stands for?"

Kip sighs, has been subjected to this game before, never knows any of the music that Cole plays. When asked, he answers that he listens to "a little bit of everything," an opinion that causes Cole to grimace and frown.

Kip pulls one of his earbuds out and half turns so he can address Cole and still print. "No, Cole, what does that stand for?"

"Millions of Dead Cops," Cole announces, a little too much glee in his voice. "Figured it was an appropriate soundtrack to the pig job you're printing." Cole crosses to their shared ink shelf, picks a glob of red plastisol ink out of a bucket with a paint scraper. He leans over Kip's press, inspects the three-color print Kip is working on. Cole is the senior printer in the shop, and it's his skill and natural talent that excuse his rough around the edges attitude, his cut off shorts, his sleeveless band tees with questionable prints on them.

"Looks good, man," Cole says, the paint scraper full of ink dangling precariously close to Kip's freshly printed shirts. "I mean, for a fascist shirt, anyway."

PRINT OR DIE

There's a yell from the end of the dryer and they both look up to see Sherry, her mouth agape. "Stop, stop, fucking stop, Kip!"

Cole flops his ink into a screen on his press and joins Sherry at the end of Kip's dryer where the police fundraiser shirts are dropping from the conveyor into a laundry basket. "Holy shit, Kip, you're fucking cooler than I thought! How'd you manage this?"

Kip swings the wheel of his press into a position that won't burn the pallets under the flash dryer and scuttles around the dryer to join them. Sherry has one of the police shirts laid out on a table, and scrawled across it in the same neon print is the word.

Pigs.

"What? Is that the test one?" Kip asks, anxiety crowding his words.

"No, Kip," Sherry says, grabbing the basket and upturning it onto the table. "It's not the fucking test shirt."

She holds up shirt after shirt, a dozen in all, all of them with *pigs* scrawled across them in the same position.

"Are you printing that in something we can't see, some discharge or glow or something?" Cole asks. He circles back to the press, spins the screens to examine them.

"I'm not printing that!" Kip says. Sweat breaks out on his forehead and he grabs his coffee mug off the top of the dryer, sips as a reflex, a nervous tick.

"When did you get a chance to burn an additional screen?" Cole asks, needling him. "Did you come in late last night or something?"

"I didn't fucking do this?"

"Do what?" Steve leans in the doorway that separates the print room from the back, his own caffeinated beverage—an iced coffee so pale Cole often chides him for it—in his meaty hand.

"Ah, fuck," Kip says, hanging his head.

"Don't be embarrassed, Kip," Cole says. "I'm fucking proud of you for taking a stand against the fascist pigs!"

Steve sighs, takes a pull from his diluted coffee. "Cole, shut the fuck up. What's going on?"

He joins Sherry at the table, sees the scrawled *pigs* across a dozen shirts, sees dollar signs dropping to the floor like rings from Sonic.

"C'mon, Kip, I can see doing one like this to appease the fucking Marxist in the corner office."

"Anarchist."

"But doing it to a dozen?"

Kip flushes, starts to speak but Steve holds up a hand. Despite his anxious nature, Steve knows the kid means well, isn't sure how this came to pass.

"Again, I could see this coming from the liberal troll over there—"

"Disestablishmentarian."

"—but from you it's honestly a surprise."

Kip looks like he wants to cry, finally spits out, "But I didn't fucking do it!"

"Listen, Kip, it's fine, we have backups of these, just take the screen down and run them right, okay? Joke's over."

"Uh, Steve?"

"Yeah, commie?"

Cole let's this misrepresentation slide. "I don't think he's doing it."

Steve joins him at the press, spins the screens, stares into each one. "Alright Kip, where's the pig screen?"

"That's what I'm telling you guys," Kip says, exasperated, "there isn't one."

"Then how . . . " Steve trails off, runs his finger gently on a screen frame.

"So you're throwing them into the dryer normal," Cole says, "and they're coming out ruined?" Even he is done joking around, the mystery more engaging than espousing some stance or political belief.

Kip shrugs, nods.

Cole prints one of the shirts on the wheel himself, flashes the base and adds the top color, then pulls it off and holds it up. "Sherry, confirm that this shirt is normal, please."

At the end of the dryer Sherry squints. "Looks right to me."

"And Steve," Cole says, turning to the boss, "please confirm that you didn't see me print *pigs,* that there is no screen with blaze orange on the press, no glow screen, no discharge screen, no screen with the word pigs on press at all."

Steve nods, looks worried, coffee sweating in his already sweaty hand.

"Alright, then here we go." Cole lays the shirt on the conveyor and Steve and Kip rush to the other side to join Sherry. "I'm staying here, watching from this side," Cole says, shooting the

JUSTIN LUTZ

shirt with the temperature gun out of habit and to add another data set to this already weird experiment. "It's hitting temp, no anomalies there."

"What the actual fuck," Sherry says. "This doesn't make any goddamn sense!" She holds up the shirt, the ink still smoking, *pigs* across it in bright orange.

"It's got to be something with the dryer, then," Kip says, getting excited, thrilled to not be at fault for this particular snafu.

"You think there's a fucking branding iron inside the dryer stamping *pigs* on the shirts you sent through?" Cole laughs. "That's fucking absurd, but in the name of science, let me try something."

He prints another shirt, holds it up for all to see, then sends it through his conveyor dryer on the other side of the room.

"Holy shit," Cole says, laughing, "whatever the fuck is doing this has a cool sense of humor." He holds up the shirt, *pigs* scrawled on it, this time in neon green.

"I don't get it at all," Sherry says, shaking her head. "I guess it has to be something . . ."

Cole, Kip, and Sherry all say it at once, their tones ranging from skeptical to excited to wary: *supernatural*.

Steve, for his part, looks nervous, sweat breaking out and running down his reddened face like heavy raindrops. "That's fucking ridiculous, I don't believe in any of that shit."

"Steve," Cole says, ignoring his skepticism and raising a squeegee in front of the boss's face like a microphone at a press conference, "can you think of any reason why your business might be haunted, and why the ghost would hate cops?"

"I'm telling you, it's not a fucking haunting—"

A noise from the back makes them fall silent, and they all hone in on it, focus on it. In the back room, completely alone, the film printer has started up, its internal works churning and grinding.

"Did you have anything in the queue?" Steve asks Sherry.

"No, I haven't been back there at all this morning," Sherry says, brow furrowed.

"It's the anti-fascist ghost communicating from beyond the grave!" Cole shouts. He grabs his coffee mug and speed walks to the back, not running so as to avoid spilling and still allowing himself to sip from the mug. The other three follow him, Kip bringing up the rear. When they arrive at the printer the film is half printed, and everyone except Cole groans.

"I fucking knew it!" Cole shouts.

Coming out of the film printer is the negative for a print of a ouija board.

***

"I don't get it, if the ghost—and I'm still not fully acknowledging that there's a ghost—but if the ghost could print this, then why doesn't it just communicate with us through the printer?"

Cole glares at Steve. "Haven't you ever seen a fucking movie, man? Where's your sense of drama, of tension?"

They're all gathered around a white t-shirt, the ouija board pattern printed on it in black ink. Cole insisted on being the one to make the screen, to print the shirt, and no one challenged him on it. Now he takes a pair of scissors and cuts the front of the shirt away so that the improvised board can lie flat on the table and pins the corners into the plastic surface.

"What are we going to use as a planchet?" Sherry asks.

"A what?"

"C'mon, Kip, you haven't seen movies either?" Cole goes to his station, roots around in a set of drawers until he finds what he's looking for and comes back to them. "This is the smallest squeegee I have," Cole says. They all stare at what he's holding, a wooden handle with a rubber blade, only two inches wide.

"Seriously?" Sherry asks.

"I mean, we can use an open box cutter, if you'd rather give the ghost a weapon," Cole says.

Sherry sighs, resigned. "Okay, how does this work?"

They move stacks of t-shirts and boxes so that they can all comfortably stand around the table and get a hand on the tiny squeegee. Steve stands a distance away, sucking on the straw of his empty coffee cup, the ice in the bottom rattling in protest.

"C'mon Steve, get in here," Cole says. We all have to summon the spirit together!" He throws the devil horns in Steve's direction, lolls his tongue out of his mouth and rolls his eyes back to the whites.

"Nah, no, no fucking way," Steve says, and turns, walks into the back room mumbling. "You act like there isn't fucking work to be done around here!" They hear his office door slam shut and they're left alone, the conveyor dryers still competing with Cole's bluetooth speaker.

Cole looks down, studies the board again. He noticed when washing out the screen that while most of it looks like the ouija boards he's grown up seeing in movies, some small elements are different. Every A and E are circled, anarchy and equality symbols respectively. Where a normal board would have "yes" and "no" in the corners, this board has them replaced with "hell yeah" and "fuck you."

"I think we have a radical ghost on our hands, gang," Cole says, his excitement rising.

"What?" Kip asks.

"Poor, innocent Kip. Are you aware of subculture at all?" Kip just stares so Cole continues, "Think of what we've seen so far. Vandalized cop shirts, now this ouija board with anarchy symbols on it? I think we're haunted with a fucking punk rock poltergeist."

Sherry groans and Kip shakes his head. "Whatever, man," Kip says. "Can we just get this over with and figured out so I can finish printing these shirts?"

"Clearly this ghost is morally opposed to the police industrial complex," Cole says. "But if you insist, captain bootlicker." He places the tiny squeegee on the fabric ouija board with shaking hands. "Alright everyone, get a hand in here." Each of them touches the squeegee and waits, expectant, but nothing happens and their fingers don't move.

"I think we have to ask it a question," Sherry says. Cole can feel her pulse beating kick drum fast in her thumbs where they touch his hands.

"So ask away," Cole says.

Sherry frowns at him, then closes her eyes. "Spirit, are you here right now?"

Cole and Kip both snort and everyone pulls their hands away from the squeegee. "What?" Sherry says, hands planted firmly on hips. "If y'all are so fucking smart then you ask it a question." Sherry's drawl peeks out from behind her professionalism when she's angry or tipsy, and that's only one of the myriad things that Cole likes about her.

"No, no," Cole says, "I'm sorry, we should be taking this seriously. That was just so adorable."

He reaches to pinch her cheeks but she slaps his hands away and looks down at the table. "Guys, what the fuck."

The squeegee, last seen in the middle of the board, now rests over "hell yeah."

"Which one of you did that?" Kip asks, a noticeable tremor in his voice.

Cole looks at Sherry, both shake their heads.

"Do you think it's in here with us?" Kip asks.

The squeegee rockets to the center of the board then slams back down onto "hell yeah."

"Holy shit holy shit holy shit," Sherry says, chants, repeats like a mantra.

"Fuck yeah," Cole says, pumping fists into the air. He's always wanted this, always been a skeptic with an open mind, waiting for the universe to show him proof. He doesn't care about the afterlife, not really, and actively despises religion, but something about this specter here with them in the shop elevates his heart rate, sends sweat to his palms, revs him up. "Our own fucking Casper, our new shop mascot!"

On the table, the squeegee slams down on "fuck you."

Kip and Sherry burst into laughter despite their fear, their nerves, their complete and total unease at having encountered the supernatural here at their day job, the one place that is supposed to be repetitive and boring and predictable.

"Guys, let's be serious," Sherry says. "We have to be respectful of the dead."

They all watch the tiny squeegee center itself on the board.

"Okay, okay," Kip says, regaining composure. "What are you here for? Do you have unfinished business?"

Without answering, the squeegee flies through the air, into the back, and slams into the door of Steve's office. They all jump back and stare, wide eyed.

"What the hell? Can we please ignore this shit and get back to work?" Steve comes into the doorway holding the squeegee and Cole wants to laugh, wants this all to be some silly lark, some weird anomaly among a life of normal days, but then he hears the rattle of the wooden squeegee handles in the rack behind him.

Live Spooky, Die Spooky.

All of the squeegees, all significantly bigger than the one that Steve holds, hurl themselves like heavy wooden javelins toward his face. He ducks, tries to run and scuttle to the floor, but they pummel into his face like wooden hammers, the rubber blades smashing into his mouth and liberating his teeth.

"Holy shit," Kip yells, and runs for the boss. Cole and Sherry follow, less enthusiastic, but the three of them manage to beat away the flying squeegees enough to drag Steve back into his office and close the door. On the other side, wood and rubber continue to beat against the door.

Steve's face is a bloody wreck, bruises already starting to bloom and sprout on his cheeks and forehead. Blood pours from his mouth and nose and he spits a tooth onto the floor. "Steve, what the fuck is this? This feels personal, no?" Cole asks.

"Guys, look at this," Sherry calls from the desk. She's in Steve's chair, looking at his computer.

"Get away from there," Steve tries to say, but it comes out garbled and messy, a bloody stew of mismatched syllables.

Kip and Cole crowd the chair while Sherry scrolls and reads.

"Heath Parker, 28, was killed Saturday in a police shootout at Wicked Ink Screen Printing, a local business run by township resident Steven Shandry. Police say they responded to a call from Shandry regarding Parker, saying he was worried for his safety and that Parker was armed and dangerous."

"Holy shit, our ghost used to work here?" Kip says.

"Steve, you cop-calling piece of shit," Cole says. He kicks the boss in the ribs and Steve rolls over on the floor, clutches at his stomach and spits blood from his ruined mouth. "Was he even armed, you fucking coward?"

Outside the office, the beating stops and they all pause, wait in the silence. It's as if the ghost, Heath Parker, is retreating, denying the story, leaving them to sort it out.

Kip reaches for the door handle but Sherry grabs his shoulder.

"C'mon," Kip says, his voice timid. "If he was killed here, there's got to be something we can do, something to appease the spirit."

"We can give him Steve," Cole says, punctuating his words with another kick. Steve groans in protest.

"We can't just let the ghost kill him," Sherry says.

"Why not? Seems like it's Steve's fault this Heath got killed, gunned down by the fascist pigs, no less," Cole says. He scratches his head for dramatic effect. "You know guys, I'm starting to realize why he was ruining the police fundraiser shirts."

Sherry rolls her eyes and Kip turns the knob, holds the door closed. "We have to be able to reason with him," he says, then pulls the door open.

There's nothing on the other side, no ghost, no squeegees.

The three of them leave Steve on the floor of his office and creep back into the print shop. On the table, the improvised ouija board is undisturbed and the squeegee planchet is back in the center of it.

"Everything looks normal, maybe he left? Maybe beating up Steve was enough?" Kip says. He steps to his press, leans down to examine the last police fundraiser shirt he printed. The wheel spins, a screen cracking his forehead open and a pallet knocking the air out of him.

Sherry runs to assist, but before she can get to him the shirt is torn from the pallet and wrapped around Kip's neck. His hands paw at his throat, trying to loosen it, but the tail of the shirt grows taut in the air as if pulled and drags him toward the conveyor dryer. Cole grabs his feet, tries to free him, but whatever cosmic force is pulling on Kip manages to get his head and neck under the guard and into the dryer, his face growing hot under the heating element.

Kip's conveyor dryer runs at seven hundred and fifty degrees, and it doesn't take long before his screams turn wet, weaken, and then stop altogether. The fight goes out of his limbs and his legs go slack in Cole's hands.

"Holy fucking hell," Cole says. He picks up a can of spray adhesive and Sherry's eyes go wide.

"Oh, good look, what are you going to do, fucking glue the ghost to death?"

"Nothing so simple," Cole says, trying to act tough. His internal monologue is screaming, his earlier fascination with the ghost turned to fear. He starts turning in circles, spraying the aerosol glue into the air.

"What the fuck," Sherry starts to say, but her words leave her when the glue clings to something in the air and forms the shape of a human, a six-foot-tall human form standing next to the dryer.

"Gotcha," Cole says, flicking his lighter in front of the can. A fireball erupts and shoots toward the incorporeal form.

"You can't fucking burn a ghost," Sherry says, stepping to take the lighter from Cole. When she gets to him something in the air pushes his hand, aims the aerosol can toward her against his will, and depresses the plunger. A ball of sticky flame shoots into Sherry's face, the glue that lands on her hair and skin acting like napalm. She falls to the ground screaming, her head and neck smoldering, and Cole steps back, drops the can, doesn't know what to do. He's alone, something he usually wants, but not like this.

Thinking quickly, he throws a hail mary pass. "Heath, if you're there, listen man, we're simpatico, we're brothers in this fight, man, I want the fascist pigs to burn too!" He turns slow circles, keeps his eyes open, and backs into his corner print station. "I want nothing but the best for you, man, if I can help you with your unfinished business, I'll do it, if you need some sort of fucking familiar or whatever here on the material plane, you've got me in your corner! Listen man, we could fuck up so many—"

His words are cut short when a boxcutter leaps from the table to find purchase in his neck.

***

Steve waits for hours, whimpering on the floor of his office, before crawling out of the puddle of blood and piss. When he manages to drag himself into the print shop, smoke fills the air and he sees Kip's headless body lying next to the conveyor dryer, the stump of his neck a smoldering mess. Sherry lies charred and blistered, all her hair gone, on the floor between presses.

At the other press, in the corner, he sees Cole still standing, looking like he does every day, standing sentinel at his workstation. He can't believe Cole would be printing shirts in this situation, that the death of his co-workers has to have rattled even a weirdo like him, and when Steve manages to work his way across the room he sees the situation for what it really is.

Cole's hand raises to his neck and pushes his head back. Half of his neck opens up like a hungry mouth and the paint scraper that he holds scoops blood and viscera from the cavity, tosses it into a screen mounted on the press.

In horror, Steve watches an invisible hand pull a squeegee, the blood filling the image burned there like ink.

The familiar becomes strange the longer you look at it.

WWW.GHOULISH.RIP

NOW AVAILABLE!

Live Spooky, Die Spooky.

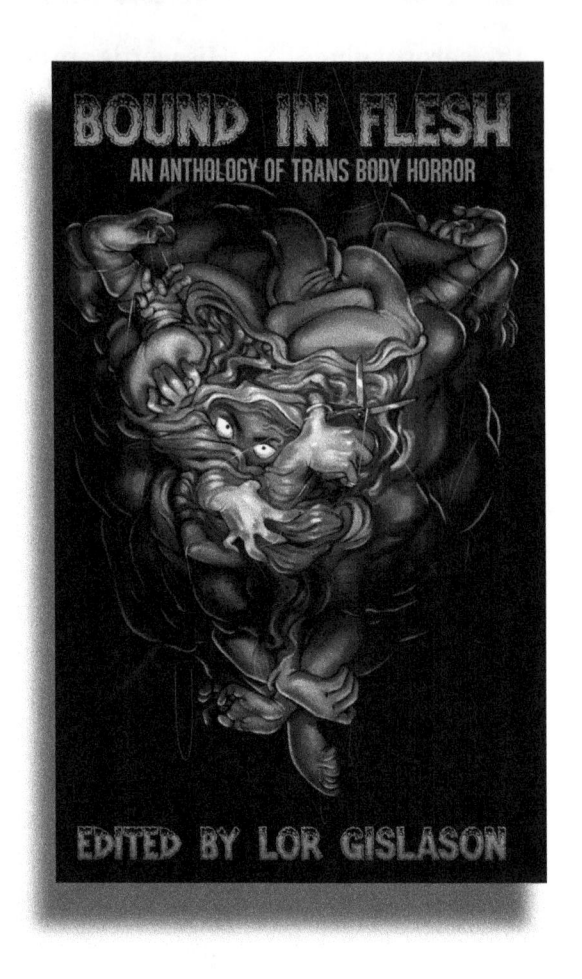

BOUND IN FLESH: AN ANTHOLOGY OF TRANS BODY HORROR BRINGS TOGETHER 13 TRANS AND NON-BINARY WRITERS, USING HORROR TO BOTH EXPLORE THE DARKEST DEPTHS OF THE GENRE AND THE BOUNDARIES OF FLESH. A DISGUSTING GOOD TIME FOR ALL! FEATURING STORIES BY HAILEY PIPER, JOE KOCH, BITTER KARELLA, AND OTHERS. EDITED BY LOR GISLASON.

AVAILABLE NOW!
WWW.GHOULISHBOOKS.COM

GOOP BY GOOP
Blobiversary Edition
Lor Gislason

WELCOME BACK TO *Goop by Goop*, where I look at some of the slimiest, wettest scenes in horror and break down how they achieved goopy perfection. As it's the 35th Anniversary of *The Blob (1988)*, what better film to take a look at? Totally not an excuse to talk about one of my favourite scenes in movie history? That's kind of what this whole series is about though so now I'm just answering my own questions.

How do you remake one of the most well-known horror films of all time? You make it really fucking gross! I genuinely believe Chuck Russell's version of *The Blob* is on par with John Carpenter's *The Thing* for super gooey special effects, not just in terms of quality, but in *variety*. Both films use every tool in the box to make their monsters move, from stop-motion to puppetry and animatronics, with each new gag one-upping the previous one. Another wild thing both films have in common is that Rob Bottin and Tony Gardner, the heads of special effects for *The Thing* and *The Blob* respectively, *were 22 years old during filming*. I could barely handle my job at McDonalds at that age.

Helming the project was Chuck Russell, who moved his way up to director after graduating from university and made his debut with *A Nightmare on Elm Street 3: Dream Warriors*—regarded by many as the best in the franchise, aside from the original. It also earned more money than the first two films *put together*, so New Line Cinema was like, yes dude, whatever you wanna do next is fine by us!

I think we're all familiar with the setup, but just in case: A weird meteorite lands near a small town and a Blob pops out, consuming everything in its path. Okay, you're caught up!

For real though: Meg (Shawnee Smith) and Paul (Donovan Leitch) have just arrived at the hospital with an injured homeless man in tow. He's got the Blob on his arm and it's *hungry*. Compared to the 50's Blob, this one moves and digests FAST. Once it grabs you—well, rest in peace buddy. While Paul's death happens early in the Blobby rampage, it's undeniably one of the more complicated set-ups and was the last sequence to be filmed.

Fun fact! During an interview with the Chicago Tribune, (*THE 23-YEAR-OLD MAN BEHIND THE BIGGEST PIECE OF SLIME IN HOLLYWOOD*, Best headline ever) described his original concept as a " . . . very pearlescent, almost like crystal sculpture" but Russell wanted more blood, so the pair compromised—each death is progressively *less* bloody, as the Blob grows and can digest things faster.

After a frantic phone call to the sheriff, The Blob (literally) jumps Paul from the ceiling. Meg hears his scream and comes running. It's about 10 seconds from this "first contact" to her seeing the result, and he's already mushy.

We cut between several rigs as Paul dissolves, including miniatures and a wax bust of Leitch that was created via digital scan using some (at the time) pretty high-tech software. The full-scale rig actually has him in there, surrounded by fibreglass for hours as they filmed this. (Russell compared it

Live Spooky, Die Spooky.

LOR GISLASON

to being waterboarded, which sounds like great fun (note I am joking)).

Both rigs consisted of a central platform with a separate "quilt" of vinyl bladders that rolled over and behind Leitch's head (nicknamed "The Waterfall"). Air compressors worked to give this movement. The Blob is meant to be an inside-out stomach, "burning, melting, and devouring almost everything it touches" so a lot of effort was put into achieving this illusion. Layers of nylon fabric, painted with veins and other details, were pulled in different directions and speeds. Pockets of the quilt were full of dyed methylcellulose, a thickening agent that would ooze out while also hiding the puppeteers underneath. This took hours to prep and was super heavy, with hundreds of pounds of slime that would stick to everyone long after they left for the day.

A fake arm attached to a "Blob Sled" was then rigged up for Smith to pull, and a crew member hit a quick-release that sent her flying backwards. The wax bust comes back into view as the head collapses, blood spewing from the eye sockets and mouth as it stretches into an agonizing scream. This scene took about a week to put together in total.

Unsurprisingly, one of the difficulties of filming was making sure all these different effects meshed together, with many shots mixing frame rates. The slime was also super reflective, so blue screens had to counteract this. It's no wonder 9 million dollars of the budget went to effects (compare this to the original, which cost about 100,000 total) and somehow they only finished the film a month before it hit theatres.

Something that really pushes horror scenes over the edge is authenticity. Smith's shocked reaction—she didn't know Leitch would be under there, just a cast—is genuine! These touches leave an unconscious impression on the viewer. Another example is the chestbuster scene in *Alien*; the cast knew what to expect, but not that real animal blood and guts were part of it. The distressing "Oh, god!" uttered by Veronica Cartwright has stuck with me ever since. We know it's fake, but the reactions make it hit home.

In the mid-2000s horror went through a resurgence of remakes, a fair amount of them bad; I was an edgy teenager, just getting into the genre, who believed only the originals were good. Obviously, I was an idiot and I freely admit this. Thank Goop for *The Blob*.

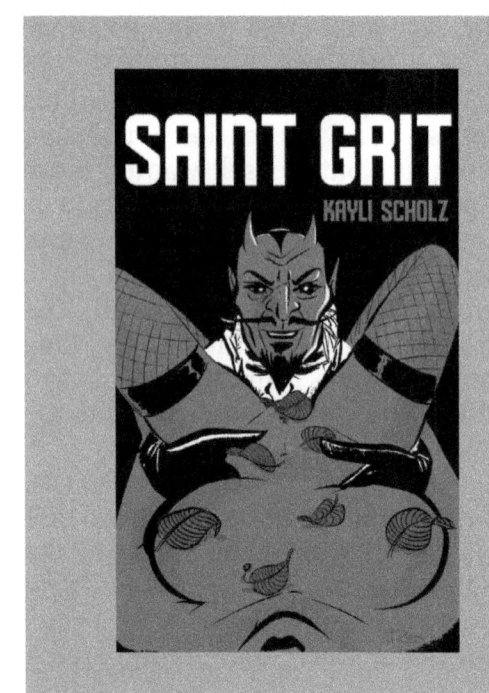

NOW AVAILABLE IN CENSORED OR UNCENSORED COVERS! WWW.GHOULISH.RIP

32

GHOULISH TALES

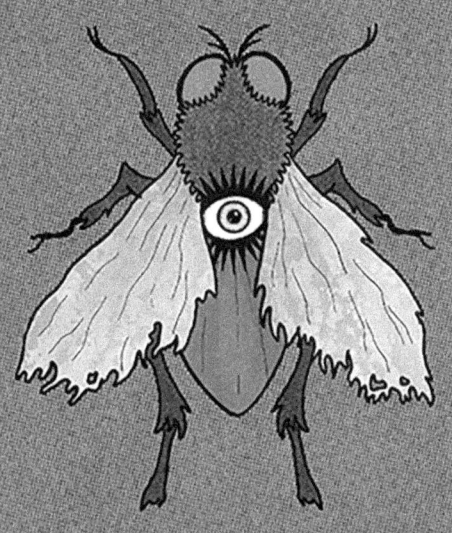

TOXICITY
MAX BOOTH III

THE MIND IS A RAZORBLADE
MAX BOOTH III

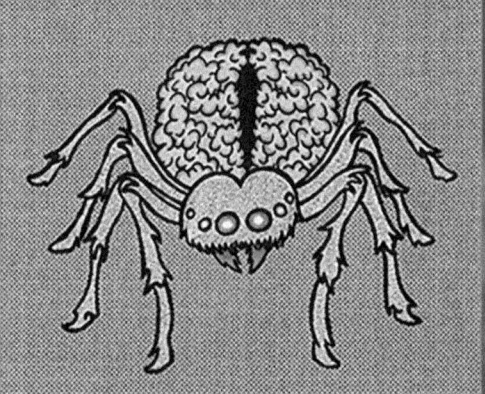

HOW TO SUCCESSFULLY KIDNAP STRANGERS
MAX BOOTH III

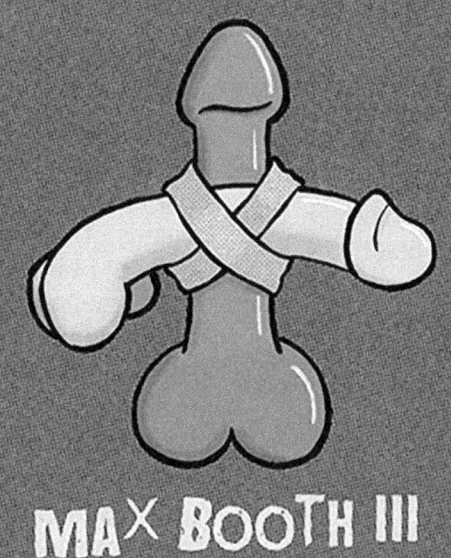

WWW.GHOULISH.RIP

A CERTAIN LEVEL OF DISCRETION

Jess Hagemann

THE WATER SLIDE corkscrews like a pale green worm from the earth it was bolted to a decade ago. It didn't make it a season before the company went bankrupt, a water park in chilly-year-round Montana a bad idea from the get-go. Now the plastic tube is faded, the wooden stairs starting to splinter as the forest attempts to swallow the bait worm of a slide. No one goes there anymore so it's where we go, Brian and I, to skateboard around the dry intestines of an empty lazy river, to tattoo each other with needles, to play with knives.

Brian gets the knives—cheap steak knives, pitted hunting knives, jumpy switchblades, flawed pocketknives with handles of inlaid bone—from his uncle, who owns a shop in town. We sit in the shadow of the old water slide and throw the knives into its belly, grown brittle from the elements. Brian's gotten really good. His arm is stronger, his aim better, and he often pierces the plastic on his first throw. Me, I'm lucky if the blade instead of the handle connects with the slide before bouncing off harmlessly. Over the past year, I've stuck one knife. Brian's landed thirty-nine. Honed from stainless steel, the half-buried blades are shiny and sharp yet as the day he acquired them.

"What if an animal falls in there?" I asked him once. "Like, down the slide and cuts itself on the blades?"

"Animals aren't that stupid," he said.

"But say it slips. A porcupine or something."

He shrugged. "That would be one unhappy porcupine."

Recalling that conversation again, the knives winking like golden quills in the setting sun, I ask, "Can porcupines shoot their quills?"

"No." He shakes his head. "That's a common misconception."

"Bummer. It would be cool if they could."

"It would be cool," he agrees.

I smile. This is why I love Brian. He knows the answer to almost everything, but it doesn't stop him from dreaming.

It gives me an idea. "I want a porcupine tattoo."

He seems to consider it, trying to picture, perhaps, what a live porcupine looks like, since the only ones we ever see are roadkill, then nods.

"Let's go up there," he says, jutting his chin toward the uppermost slide platform. The trees haven't quite overtaken it and there's more light.

Quietly, we stand and dust our jeans off, begin climbing the rotting wood stairs. We skip the treads that are broken or missing, remember not to grip the railing where the hungry points of nails poke through. From the top we can see to the Crazies, their peaks a dark purple against the horizon. I take a photo with my mind. Although we tell ourselves home has nothing to offer us, I cannot deny its rugged beauty.

"Take off your pants," Brian says, and I do. I leave them where they fall and step toward the platform corner, where I assume a new seat and rest my back against a post. Brian takes our kit from his backpack, selects a needle, tears open a moist towelette. As he wipes the needle down he asks me where I want it and I point to a spot on my upper thigh between the cross he gave me last

A CERTAIN LEVEL OF DISCRETION

month and the compass rose that's still scabbed over. It's one of the few places on my body my dad won't see. Being a pastor's kid requires a certain level of discretion.

Even though Brian's technique has greatly improved since we began this game, I still grunt at the first prick of needle into skin. A buzzy, nervy pain shoots through me and I try not to squirm, but it's like he is digging. "Jesus," I say through gritted teeth, "that really hurts."

"It's the quills," he says. "I have to connect the dots into lines or it won't look like a porcupine."

To distract myself, I disassemble the dollar-store pen, removing the barrel of black ink and preparing to crack it open.

Brian sighs and rocks back on his heels. "I think I need a knife."

I go cold. Goosebumps pimple my naked legs. "Why?"

"Just little cuts," he says. "For the quills."

He finds one he hasn't thrown into the slide at the bottom of his bag. It has a nick in the blade near its handle, which made it unsellable. I watch Brian clean it.

As he brings the blade tip toward my thigh, I stop breathing. I chew on the inside of my cheek and concentrate on his hairline so I don't look at how he's mutilating me. His hair is dyed the color of lava rock, the faux burgundy obvious above his light eyebrows. As I look, beads of perspiration appear. He's nervous, too, and this realization excites me.

When the blade slips into my flesh, parting it like lips, I think again that I love him and grow hard. It's an instinct, a reflex, not something I meant to happen, and with his face that close to my groin Brian cannot miss it. He freezes. I tense up. "Shit," I say, scrambling to grab my jeans to cover my boxers. "Shit, I'm sorry."

"No worries," he says, breezy, though I can tell this development at least is something he doesn't know the answer to.

Brian stands up, not looking at me. I need him to look at me, to say it's all right. "Brian," I say. I reach for him. "Brian—"

Brian isn't stupid, but in the end he is an animal. When I reach for him, he steps backward, an equal and opposite reaction. The rubber sole of his shoe catches on a weather-warped plank and he stumbles. He tries to regain his balance but only trips over his backpack. I grab at his jeans like I can stop him, then he's gone, swallowed by the bait worm being swallowed by the woods.

He doesn't scream until he hits the first of the knives. They cut far deeper into his legs than he cut me. His strong arms try to grip one but the blade takes off his fingers. He yanks his hand to his chest protectively and curls around it in time to slide over the only blade I managed to stick, making him Jesus pierced by Pilate. Which makes me Pilate.

My dad's voice comes unbidden into my head. *Was Pontius Pilate a good guy or a bad guy?* he quizzes us from the lectern. *He turned Jesus over to the soldiers who killed him, but he was just doing what the people wanted. And if you believe the prophets, what God himself had preordained. So maybe on the spectrum of good to evil, Pilate wasn't either . . . but the fulcrum on which fate turned, the tool that carried out God's will.*

I drag Brian, bleeding and dizzy, from the bottom of the slide where he lies crumpled to the passenger seat of his old Jeep Wrangler and help him in. We tear out of the gravel parking lot and toward the hospital, a twenty-minute drive we finish in twelve. On the way I don't say anything; neither does he. It's not until I screech to a halt outside the ER doors that I realize I'm still in my underwear. I dump Brian into a waiting wheelchair, jump back in the jeep, and drive off, a porcupine doing the impossible: shootings quills into his best friend's back, calling it fate, calling it an accident, never speaking of it again.

WEEKEND-LONG BOOK FESTIVAL FOR HORROR FANATICS

MARCH 15, 16, 17

SPOOKY BOOKSTORE!

LIVE READINGS!

PANELS!

HORROR CONTESTS!

GHOULISH BOOK FESTIVAL 2024

525 S. ST MARYS, SAN ANTONIO

GHOULS OF HONOR
JESSICA MCHUGH • DANIEL KRAUS • RJ JOSEPH

EVENT HOURS: FRI 1PM-9PM | SAT 10AM-11PM | SUN 10AM-3PM
SPOOKY BOOKSTORE FREE TO THE PUBLIC
BOOKSTORE HOURS: FRI 12PM-6PM | SAT 10AM-6PM | SUN 10AM-5PM
BADGES FOR PANELS AND LIVE READINGS AVAILABLE!
WWW.GHOULISH.RIP

THE ONE WITH THE GAS STATION

Shannon Riley

"**No, I've told you**, that fucking show is unfunny and way too overhyped. I'm not watching it," Dante groaned into the cordless, emerging from the back room and rubbing the chill from his hands. He pushed what he could of his wet hair behind his ears. Over the speakers he heard the chorus to a TLC song, which should have annoyed him but didn't.

"You asshole," came Joe's tinny voice from the earpiece. "I watched all of *Twin Peaks* for you. That show was weird as shit. I've been telling you to watch it for months now, the least you can do is give it a try."

Dante rubbed his bare arms together for warmth. Goosebumps had started to form on the clammy flesh of his soft triceps. The gas station notoriously didn't hold in heat very well, which sucked during this time of year. Careful not to slip on the wet linoleum, Dante passed through the aisle directly in front of him, candy bars on the left, bags of chips on the right, and toward the front counter. In one sweeping motion he snatched a bag of pretzels from the end cap and tore it open with his front teeth.

"Dude, I *have* watched it," he replied through a mouthful of pretzel, "I saw like the first five episodes and it just never got any better."

He passed by the counter and through the hip-height swinging door that opened into the station's cash wrap. The space was small, maybe six feet by three feet, but adequate as far as convenience stores go. Nestled against the outdated register were a few stands for lighters, a revolving carousel of sunglasses, and a mostly empty tip cup. Dante leaned over and fished out what had generously been left inside the cup: a crumpled receipt, a wet, discarded gum wrapper, and a nickel. He stuffed another handful of pretzels into his mouth, shoved his hand into his pocket, and retrieved a couple of dollars that he placed in the cash register. A small black radio sat against the Rolo display. Along the back wall, smokes and tinned tobacco. Dante positioned himself loosely behind the cash register, leaned against the counter, and flipped on the radio.

"And there's just no reason for the episodes to all be named the same thing," he continued, balancing the cordless between his shoulder and ear as he tuned the radio to one of the local stations covering the weather. "It's just a cutesy gimmick."

"They're not all called the *same* thing," argued Joe from the phone.

"Close enough," Dante replied. "Anyway, they're just all bad characters. Once Maggie Wheeler was introduced I had to bounce, sorry. Hey, hold on a second."

Dante got the radio tuned correctly, and the authoritative voice of the anchor floated from the speaker, crackling slightly through the static. He peered out the windows on the other side of the register at the growing snowstorm outside.

" . . . minimum temperatures reaching twelve degrees in the northern counties, and as low as nine degrees here in Sussex County alone. Expect snowfall to accumulate at one inch per hour. Average winds will be southwest and reach speeds of thirty miles per hour . . ."

SHANNON RILEY

From his view behind the register, he could see very little except the sky, which was blown out to a near white from the snowfall. Evening was approaching, and what little remained of the sun shone through heavy, low clouds that felt close enough for Dante to touch.

" . . . reduced visibility will impact road travel, so drivers should execute increased caution when traveling on motorways, and be sure to alert emergency services to any abandoned or disabled vehicles. Listeners can report accidents, road hazards, or other emergency contingencies by contacting the station directly at—"

Dante switched the radio off.

He rubbed his eyes with the palm of his free hand. "Are you following this storm?" he said to Joe.

"Yeah," Joe replied, "they're saying it's coming in faster than anyone expected. No one could plan ahead for it, so now everyone's scrambling. Even more reason why you've got to tell George to stick this shift up his ass and cut loose. You don't see his ass volunteering to work the blizzard shift."

"I don't know, man." Dante rolled his eyes. Every other conversation he had with Joe about his job eventually concluded with Joe telling Dante how much of an asshole his boss was, and that he should walk out, middle fingers cocked, and tell George all the unpleasant things he'd do to his mother if she wasn't confined to a nursing home. But Dante had to give Joe a little bit of credit here, he wasn't wrong about the blizzard.

Dante pushed out away from the counter and walked around to the front door. He switched the cordless to the other ear and pressed himself against the glass. The station was set off apart from the highway, about a quarter mile off of exit 77. From Dante's perspective, he could see the wide, flat paved lot with its neat row of pumps and modest parking area just to the left of the entrance. Beyond that, the view merely consisted of a glowing Burger King sign peeking out over a dense thatch of trees down over the neighboring hillside.

The snow had fallen for the past few hours, but had really only picked up after Dante clocked in. Tire marks from the Toyota that rolled in forty minutes ago had filled in now. Every passing minute, the station disappeared more and more deeply in blinding white obscurity.

"What don't you know? Just leave, man. No one's out in this weather, anyway."

"I told you," Dante sighed, "I can't leave. Marco dropped me off in his Comanche since mine is about six months past due on its oil change and finally starting to make noises."

"And he can't come get you?"

"No, dude." He felt a hangnail on his thumb, and stuck the finger in his mouth to chew it off. "He has his own job to get to. He was going to come pick me up again at midnight."

Joe sighed into Dante's ear. "Whatever."

Dante scoffed. "Your ass is so worried, why don't you come get me?"

"I can't even if I wanted to. My mom's making me watch their dog for the weekend. I'm kind of stuck here."

Dante craned his head to try to see past the parking lot and onto the main road, cheek pressing against the frigid glass. "How's it by your house?"

"The roads have gone to shit. Jess almost got herself stuck driving back from Pathmark."

Dante grinned, and allowed the smile to make its way into the tone of his voice. "Yeah? How *is* your sister, by the way?"

Dante had always liked Jess. They went to high school together back in the day and talked a lot about horror movies and their love of Danzig. They went to basement shows a few times a month, and they'd trade off sharing music that came out of the Jersey scene, because there was always plenty of new stuff to go around. There was a brief period of time where the two of them may have been a thing, but Dante had long since gotten over her. Now mostly he just weaponized their will-they-or-won't-they dynamic against Joe, who never failed to voice his discomfort about the subject.

"Hey, fuck off, she doesn't date college drop outs."

"At least I got a job."

"That's a stretch and you know it. They'd have canned your ass if you weren't the only one that remembered to fill the coffee maker."

The coffee maker, damn.

"Oh, that reminds me," he said, giving one final scan of the empty parking lot before turning to the coffee station. Joe was right, he was the only one who gave a damn about the coffee, most likely because he was guilty of finishing half a pot over

THE ONE WITH THE GAS STATION

the course of his own shift. But the customers liked it, too, and he liked the busy work and the smell of a fresh cup.

"Seriously though, tell her I said hi."

"I won't."

Dante shook his head, wedged the cordless between his ear and shoulder, and began scooping grounds into a fresh filter. The coffee was almost out, he'd have to remember to get another can from the back.

At that moment, from behind, the shrill bell above the front entrance rang out, slicing through the silence of the store. His guts twisted and his heart fell into his stomach, an embarrassing yelp burping out from a high place in his throat. In his surprise he spun around to face the door, and in doing so, sent both the coffee filter and the cordless phone flying. The phone slid along the linoleum, disappearing somewhere behind the Lay's display.

In the open doorway was a man, older than Dante, but probably not as old as his clothing made him appear. He wore thick work pants and heavy work boots, both covered in a thick layer of crusted snow. His eyes were wide and bright, standing out from behind wiry red eyebrows and a tangled beard. His cheeks were flush. He wasn't wearing a coat, but he didn't look cold. He said nothing, only stared directly at Dante, who was now covered in a fine layer of coffee dust.

Dante looked down at his pants, still soaked and cold, and now caked with brown coffee grounds. He tried to brush it away, but it clung to the wet fabric of his jeans. Resolutely he sighed and returned his gaze to the stranger, who was still staring at him, unblinking and silent.

"Sorry, man, you startled me," Dante said, his pulse slowly settling. "I was just looking out the window and I didn't see anyone out there, you kind of snuck up on me."

For a moment, Dante didn't think the stranger was going to say anything back. For a beat longer than what seemed normal, the man only stared in Dante's direction, mouth slightly agape, clothing silently dripping on the linoleum. Dante wondered if the man had been in some kind of accident or was otherwise just incapable of speech, when he finally opened his mouth and spoke.

"I have a flat tire," he said, in a flat, wooden tone.

Dante nodded and offered the man a sympathetic shrug. "Ah, tough break, man," he said. "Where were you headed in this weather?"

"Can you help me?"

Dante rubbed his palms on a dry patch of his pants and turned back to the coffee counter to clean the mess he had made. "Uh, I can try. What do you need?"

"Can you come with me and help me?"

Dante turned back to the man, who, despite carrying on a conversation, regardless of how stilted and foreign the flow may have been, stood in a way that conveyed utter discomfort engaging in any human interaction. His knees were locked tight, his shoulders slumped, and still, that unfaltering eye contact. The more Dante looked, the less sure he was that this man was well.

"Dude," he said, suddenly very aware of how vulnerable he was, isolated, and alone. "Are you alright? Do you want me to call someone for you?"

"Can you come with me?" the stranger repeated, ignoring the concern.

Joe's tinny voice rang out from the cordless on the floor, calling out in confused, worried, and otherwise indecipherable tones. Dante resisted the urge to step forward to fish it out from under the chip display, which would close the gap between him and the man in the door.

"Come *with* you?"

The stranger nodded. "Can you come with me?"

Even now, the man's posture didn't change, didn't shift. He stood, wooden and locked still, unnatural in his skin, jaw clenched but still projecting clearly, voice ringing through the store.

"No, sorry," Dante replied.

"So you won't come with me?"

"No," he repeated, now trying to cut the irritation bubbling upward. "Man, I'm working. I'm by myself here, I can't leave."

The stranger didn't reply.

He continued to drip on the linoleum. Dante was going to need to get the wet floor sign from the back.

"Listen, if you need somewhere to hang until the storm passes, you can sit inside here or something. Have some coffee," he offered reluctantly, despite the gnawing feeling to get the man out of there. "But I can't leave."

Live Spooky, Die Spooky.

Joe's voice continued to ring out from the floor. At this, the stranger's eyes darted in the direction of the cordless. His eyes widened, as though piercing facts of a case together or solving a brain teaser. Some unknowable instinct tangled in Dante's guts then, and it struck him how desperately he did not want this man to find the phone.

"Look," Dante said, "the phone in here isn't for customer use but there's a payphone on the other side of the station, right next to the bathroom, if you want to use it."

Dante barely got the words out of his mouth before the stranger turned on the spot, pushed the door open, and exited the store. With purpose, he turned left and strode past the window, into the storm, and out of sight. As his brain tried to work out what had just happened, Dante remained frozen in place for one beat, two beats, before hurrying forward, crouching and reaching for the cordless, and jamming it to his ear.

"Joe! Hey, are you still there?"

"Dante, what the fuck happened?"

Dante rushed forward to the door, put his face as close as possible to the glass, and craned his neck to try to follow where the stranger had walked off to. The briefest flash of brown fabric disappeared around the corner, leading to the back of the building, toward the bathroom and payphone.

Dante explained as best he could to Joe exactly what had occurred, but the gravity of the weirdness was desperately lost in translation.

"So the guy just had a flat tire and needed the phone?"

"No," Dante sighed, flinging his hand uselessly in the air in front of him, "I mean, yes, that's what he said, but you should have seen him, he was so . . . " He paced up and down the beef jerky aisle, running his hands through his hair. "He was so weird, and now he's just disappeared."

With every gust of wind that rattled the front door, Dante snapped his head toward the sound, to only be once again met with blinding whiteness and nothing more.

Later, Dante was refilling bags of trail mix and setting a mental reminder to no longer allow George to have any control over the radio station. If he had to hear another Hootie song during this shift, he was definitely going to be shoving a Slim Jim into one of his very own precious ear canals

The hanging bell over the front door rang out, and Dante leapt up to peer over the aisle. Taut piano wire tightened in his guts, fearing the return of the bearded stranger. But in the doorway this time wasn't a tall, wiry, stoic man. This time, there was a woman.

It was Jess.

Dante's cheeks prickled with rushing blood at the welcome sight of Joe's sister. His chest tightened, and his heart thumped violently against his sternum. He hadn't seen her in months. She looked beautiful and bright and although her being here made no sense, man was he grateful to see her all the same. Just as he was about to open his mouth to exclaim a greeting, he stopped himself.

It wasn't Jess.

Dante blinked and looked again. The woman looked so much like Jess, she could have been a sister. A fraternal twin. He simultaneously saw Jess and Not–Jess, like looking at an optical illusion and trying to see both pictures at the same time. She looked similar, but not quite right. Like someone had tried to mold Jess from memory, but somewhere the details got lost. Like Jess, the girl was short, with a round face and an angular nose. Her hair, long and wet, hung lifelessly along the sides of her face. She wore a long-sleeved shirt, denim jeans, and sneakers. No coat, no hat, and everything was caked in snow. Her skin was pale, sickly and blueish, except the tomato red tip of her nose. Her eyes darted around the store until they met Dante's.

He swallowed before managing, "Hi, can I help you?"

"I have a flat tire," she said, in monotone.

A sour feeling twisted in his throat, and Dante cautiously came around the front of the aisle, still clutching a bag of peanuts. Even her voice sounded like Jess. Except the way she looked back at him, it was like there was nothing behind her eyes. She looked right through him.

"A flat tire?" he repeated, not sure he heard correctly.

"Can you help me?"

Dante was struck by the bizarre parallel, felt disquiet at the uncomfortably similar exchange of conversation. Either she was with the man from

THE ONE WITH THE GAS STATION

earlier, or the two of them had found themselves in a statistically impossible scenario. Dante didn't believe such a coincidence was possible. The woman continued to stare through Dante, looking weak and pale and ill.

"Miss, are you okay?" Dante asked, afraid to come any closer. She was soaked from the snow, but looked entirely unaffected by it.

"Can you come with me?" she asked.

Dante was struck with the sick realization that he wanted her to leave, no matter how ill prepared for the weather she was. His stomach tightened at the idea of refusing her; her resemblance to Jess was still so haunting, it would be like turning his very own loved one onto the street.

"Are you with that guy? The one with the beard? Are you in trouble?"

She ignored the question and repeated herself. "Can you come with me and help?"

"No!" Dante croaked out. He stomped his foot like a child. "I'm not going anywhere, I'm not leaving here! You need to get your own help, understand?"

She didn't relinquish the unsettling eye contact, and for a few seconds, Dante was afraid she was going to do something crazy, like pounce at him. He'd have no defenses except for his size. He certainly couldn't get anyone out here to help if she and her boyfriend did something to him. Just as quickly as the thought had entered Dante's mind and he was plotting out emergency solutions, Not–Jess turned in a perfect half-circle, and promptly let herself out the front. She turned left down the side of the building and disappeared from view, displacing the tall snow as she went.

Dante ran forward and locked the door behind her.

He debated for ten minutes on whether or not he should call someone. He sat, pressed up against the store's far wall, chewing on his hangnail, and rubbing his forehead against the cordless phone he snatched up as soon as she had left. His eyes never left the front door. Every time a gust of wind sent debris flying past the window, Dante's breath would catch and send his heart into his throat. The sun was setting, and what little visibility he had waned by the minute.

He would just call Joe to chat. It didn't have to be anything. Dante was bored, Joe was bored, they could just talk and pass the time. Dante would mention what had happened and they would both laugh at how lame he was, and everything would feel normal again.

Dante lifted the phone to dial Joe's number, when the phone rang. He nearly shit himself.

After his heart attack receded, he answered as professionally as he could.

"Dante?"

"Joe? Man, I was just about to call you."

"Dante, you need to come outside," he said.

The unsettled feeling pulsed in Dante's guts again. Acid rose up in his throat, burning. He tried to swallow it away. A throbbing had begun in the space behind his eyes.

"Joe?"

"Come outside," Joe repeated.

He didn't sound right. His voice sounded normal, but something hitched in his tone, disrupting his cadence. His delivery felt unnatural, like he was being held at gunpoint and reciting a handwritten ransom speech written by a captor. But Joe didn't sound anxious or desperate. He sounded dull and deadpan, tired even.

"Joe, where are you?"

"I'm outside," Joe said. "Jess is here. She needs your help."

Jess? Joe pushed himself to standing, stuck the phone between his ear and shoulder, and wrapped his arms around his middle.

"What's wrong?"

"Dante, you just have to come outside. We need you."

"How did you get here?" He avoided moving closer to the door, but squinted into the darkening parking lot. He didn't see any cars outside.

"Dante, she called me from the payphone. She told me how weird you were to her in the store, like you didn't recognize her. And now she's in trouble, come outside and meet us."

Nothing made sense. That woman wasn't Jess. Unless, was it? Was something wrong with *him*? If that was Jess, why couldn't he recognize her? What was happening to him? Dante felt dizzy and cold and more than a little paranoid, and despite any and all signals in his body screaming at him to *not*, Dante ran forward, threw the door open, and forced himself out into the cold. The wind caught him, and his hair whipped violently into his face

Live Spooky, Die Spooky.

and eyes, stinging like little needles. The shockingly frigid air sucked the breath out of him. His sneakers sunk into the snow, now halfway up his calves. Dante looked out over the parking lot and saw nothing, only white blankness and raging snow. He squinted left along the station's exterior, as far as he could until the corner turned and there was nothing left to see. From beyond the corner he could hear sounds, sharp and ringing out over the wind.

The phone was back to his ear and he cried out, "Where are you?" His voice cracked with the effort.

Joe's voice rang out clearly, "We're behind the building, Dante. Turn left and come around the corner."

Dante ignored the niggling feeling that Joe should have no idea where Dante was at that moment in order to instruct him to turn in a specific direction. Despite the pain of the cold and the acid in his gut telling him to turn the other direction and run, he found himself propelled forward. He didn't think Joe and Jess were anywhere near the building anymore. But he just needed to *see*. He reached the corner of the building, and although the cautious thing would have been to take pause, to collect his thoughts, to plan for whatever he may find, instead he barreled around the bend, propelled by fear and by cold and by the realization that he couldn't just sit and wait for the nightmare to find him.

Through the flying snow and the darkening skies, he saw it.

Huge and black and bubbling, it clung wetly to the backside of the building. It was in motion, alive, but unlike any living organism Dante had seen. It stuck, leechlike, and heavy, to the wall, throbbing rhythmically. Although from the rhythm of a pulse or of breath, Dante couldn't tell. He craned his neck to take it in, and as he did, he saw the translucent, pulsing flesh and the constant liquid movement within. It was full of everything. Dante watched as faces pushed out from the slick membrane, and then were sucked back in, indistinguishable from each other and passive in expression. And the sounds, Dante could hear every sound layered on top of each other, a symphony of honking horns, braying animals, metal on metal, phones ringing, screaming, whispering, laughter. From somewhere in the depths he swore he heard his own name calling back out to him.

He knew instantly the storm brought it here.

Or.

He knew instantly that it brought the storm.

He knew it wanted him.

He didn't know anything.

He knew he had to get away.

Dante tried to step back, but his shoe caught in a chunk of ice and the momentum sent him falling backward and into the snow. If the creature hadn't noticed him before, it certainly did now. The mass shifted closer to Dante, reaching toward him, and releasing from the side of the building. As it moved, it made a thick, sucking sound that turned Dante's bowels into water. Despite its massive size, it moved quickly and efficiently, and if he didn't get up now, it would be on him in seconds. Dante clawed his way back to his feet, now utterly soaked, and ran.

His jeans hung heavy as he moved through the snow, knees high, through the parking lot, past the gas pumps, and onto the main road. He could hear the sounds of the mass behind him, but he refused to turn. He knew if he stopped, if he turned, if he even looked, it would be over. He didn't want to know how it moved, how horrible it would have looked. All in one, biological and alien, yet composed entirely of humanity, and coming, coming for him. Somewhere deep inside of him, he made the passive observation of how quiet he was. He didn't scream, he didn't call for help. His gasping breaths echoed in his ears, and his eardrums pulsed with blood.

He was still holding the cordless.

He put it up to his ear, and Joe's voice rang out, clearer than it had ever been, as though it was coming directly from inside Dante, "Dante you need to come back."

"I won't," he gasped, lungs burning as he ran.

"Jess is here with us, and she needs you."

A red light that Dante hadn't noticed before shone from the side of the cordless: OUT OF RANGE.

"That's not her! And that's not you!" he screamed into the cordless anyway.

"Dante, she loves you, and I approve. Come back and we can make things right."

Dante forced the phone away from himself, but

THE ONE WITH THE GAS STATION

couldn't release it from his frozen grasp. He raced down the hill and onto the exit ramp, lungs on fire, and feet faltering at the speed, threatening to send him to the ground. The rumbling grew behind him, and fear pricked at his neck. Still he kept both eyes forward and forward and only forward.

Suddenly the rumbling was so loud, it was inside of him. The ground shook, the snow displaced mere feet behind him, crunching under the weight. He sensed the huge, dark mass inches to his left, and he finally was forced to turn and see.

The snow plow had come to a stop next to him, a chance at rescue. He could get himself onto the highway and back home, and get Joe and Jess to safety. With numb fingers he clawed open the door. The interior of the plow was pitch black and so warm. He felt the heat against his cheek as he hoisted himself up and in, toward safety and salvation.

The inside was larger than it appeared from the outside, flat and wide and warm. He walked straight in, allowing the heat of the cab to sink into his flesh, for the blood to rush back to his extremities. The tip of his nose and the rounds of his cheeks tingled with the sensation, and his mouth was full of spit and snot. He was soaked wet, freezing, but alive, and so grateful for it.

He spoke aloud in the direction of the driver, but kept the cordless to his ear. He couldn't remove it yet, his fingers frozen tight on the cheap plastic.

"Thank you so much for picking me up, I thought I was gonna die out there."

The driver didn't answer, but Dante didn't care. He was rescued, safe, and was never going back to the station to face what was hidden in the storm again.

He continued onward, moving through the plow's interior, deeper and deeper, through the hallway and passing by the storage closets and the back office. In the distance he could make out the music coming from the cab, floating over his head. A TLC song, this one wasn't so bad, Dante supposed. George has certainly picked worse stations.

Joe's voice returned to Dante's ear, at first full of static, but then sharper and sharper until—

"Have you started *Friends* yet or not?"

As much media as the two of them had shared over the years, he still found himself annoyed on the occasion that Joe would recommend something safe and saccharine and totally out of sorts with what Dante was into. He rolled his eyes.

"No, I've told you, that fucking show is unfunny and way too overhyped. I'm not watching it." He emerged from the back room and into the fluorescence of the main convenience area, shaking off the wet that had accumulated in his hair. He was struck by how cold he was and fruitlessly rubbed his palms on his jeans, only to find they were wet, too. The disquiet scratched somewhere for him, deep at the base of his skull, but he brushed it away because there was work to be done here.

Live Spooky, Die Spooky.

IN DREAMS WE ROT

BETTY ROCKSTEADY

FICTION LIKE A FEVER DREAM

A voyeur becomes the one being watched, terrifying beasts are stitched together, strange new insects appear, ancient sex gods rise, and an island on the brink of madness falls apart.

Betty Rocksteady's debut collection blends surrealism and horror, tearing apart tropes as words bleed and transform down unexpected avenues of nightmare logic. These stories run the gamut from splatterpunk to somber. They're hot and wet and nasty, guaranteed to leave you with an unspeakable sense of dread

WWW.GHOULISH.RIP

Would you really want your book to look like this?

No, of course not!

You've worked hard to complete your masterpiece.

Make it look as professional as you are.

www.TheAuthorsAlley.com

HAIR PROBLEMS

Danger Slater

ONE TIME THIS GUY tried to carjack me. True story.

It was after midnight on a weekday. Out near the suburbs.

Most people were already in bed. Front doors locked. TVs turned off. Alarm clocks set for work in the morning. Asleep. Most people had no reason to be driving around after midnight. Most people didn't know or care what the air tasted like on this side of the moon.

I was stopped at a red light when this man came up to my window and tapped on the glass. I yelped. I was not expecting a man to tap on my glass. Perhaps I should have been more vigilant but I rolled the window down. This was the safest part of the city, I'd been told. I had nothing to worry about out here. And regardless of what part of the city I was in, if a stranger needed my help, I strove to be the kind of person who would help them anyway. I'm a nice guy, even if people haven't always been nice to me in the past. Believe it or not, I used to have a lot of anger problems when I was younger. Whenever I was confronted with some kind of challenge I couldn't overcome I used to scream and cry and punch holes in the drywall. I was a real asshole, I'll admit without shame. But these days I've learned to process my emotions in a much healthier manner. I exercise regularly. I eat fruits and vegetables. I have a black cat named Bubbles who sits on my lap and keeps me in line. I have learned that you relinquish your power when you get angry. No matter how strong you think you are, your anger will always be stronger. Even when you get your way, even when you get results, if you allow yourself to be controlled by your anger, you still lose in the end.

So I thought maybe this guy needed directions. Maybe he could use a couple bucks for a cup of coffee or hot meal. Maybe he recognized me and wanted an autograph. I am a marginally famous fiction writer in some niche online circles. I've been recognized once or twice.

But when I saw that vacant, tweaker-hungry look in his eyes I knew I had made an egregious mistake. This was a desperate and dangerous man who was about to do a desperate and dangerous thing.

He had a hunting knife on him. Something he probably stole from some tool shed somewhere. He brandished the thing inches from my nose, so close I could see my reflection warping around the edge of the blade.

"Get out or I will stab you," he said to me.

"Okay, okay," I said. "I'm getting out, let's just be cool."

Some days I wonder if I've made a mistake letting my anger go so readily. I wonder if I should've held onto that part of myself just a little while longer, those last few drops of fuel in my soon-to-be empty gas tank. There was a certain degree of clarity that came with my anger. Things were much sharper when I refused to let ambiguity cloud my vision. Life is dangerous and unpredictable and so many things were beyond my control. They say that even the stars in the sky will burn out in time. So I wonder, should I be worried about the eventual heat death of the universe?

HAIR PROBLEMS

Should I try to save the whales? Should I stop and smell the roses? What was the point of doing anything at all?

I made like I was going to turn off the ignition but instead I threw the car back into drive and pressed the pedal to the floor. Engine revving. Tires squealing. Exhaust pipe coughing up smoke. I sped away, screaming fuck youuuuuuu at the top of my lungs, my would-be marauder left standing in the middle of the darkened street, ineffectual knife held out in front of him like his limp little dick in his stubby-fingered hand.

***

Shortly after the carjacking incident, I noticed my hair starting to fall out. Just a few strands at first. Collecting in the shower drain. Nothing to be alarmed about, I thought. But soon it escalated. I'd find clumps of hair on my pillow in the morning. On the shoulders of my jacket. Filling the lint trap in the dryer. I could see it in the bathroom mirror while I brushed my teeth. The slight change in my appearance. All this extra forehead. There was no denying what was happening. I was balding. And fast.

So I booked an appointment with my primary care physician, Dr. Alexandra McMannequin, to see if we couldn't Sherlock Holmes our way to the bottom of this. Perhaps this was symptomatic of some kind of underlying health issue. Perhaps it could be reversed. Perhaps my hair loss had nothing to do with the fact that I recently celebrated my 40th birthday. It was an unceremonious affair. Bought myself a frosted cupcake. Got a text from my mother. Took an extra-long bath. But other than that it was a day like any other. Were I to go bald I knew it wouldn't be the biggest tragedy in the world. These kinds of things happen to Men of a Certain Age. There are lots of guys out there who have already completed that leg of their Gentleman's Journey. But it wasn't so much the change in aesthetic that concerned me, as it was the implication of what this change might mean. I was getting older. And there wasn't much I could do to stop it.

I sat on the examination table in the middle of an antiseptic white office. Opposite the doctor. On her stool. Legs crossed. Glasses on. Jotting every word I said down on the clipboard she held in her hands.

"Dr. McMannequin, I'm losing my hair and I'm worried it might mean I have cancer or something. I'm freaking out over here. And I can't stop going to the bathroom, either. I hafta pee every five minutes. Are these two things related? Why is this happening to me?"

The doctor inspected my scalp like she was searching it for seams.

"Well it doesn't appear to be falling out to me," she said as she once again took her seat. "In fact, at a glance, I'd say you have more hair than normal. Especially for a person your age. More so than my husband, that's for sure. He's as bald as a cue ball, but he's still sexy as hell. There are lots of hot bald guys. I can think of ten just off the top of my head. My husband looks exactly like Bruce Willis in his prime. You, on the other hand, have this kind of neurotic Woody Allen thing going on, which I'm sure I needn't remind you is problematic in and of itself. I don't care that he made *Annie Hall*. That dude is gross."

"It's not so much the overall visual presentation that worries me, doctor. It's the density. It's a lot less dense than it was a mere decade ago. If this is the start of the balding process for me, I'm left to wonder, when and where will this madness end?"

"Do you have a picture of yourself from a decade ago we could reference?" she asked. "It'll be hard to establish a baseline without anything to compare it to."

I opened my Instagram feed. Scrolled backward. Dr. McMannequin leaned in. Over my shoulder. So close her floral perfume overtook my senses. Like lilacs, I thought, even though I had no idea what lilacs actually smelled like. I've walked this Earth for 40 years and I don't even know the first thing about lilacs.

Scrolling. Down the feed. My life as I'd lived it thus far, unfurled against my thumbs. Dr. McMannequin and I were travelers through time. 2020. 2018. 2017. And further back still. All the way to 2014. The year I first downloaded the app.

I stopped on a photograph of my ex-girlfriend and I decorating the apartment we used to share for Halloween.

"That's a cool jack-o-lantern," Dr. McMannequin said.

"Thanks," I replied. "My ex carved it. I'm not very artistic. It's supposed to be my cat."

"Yeah, I can see it. With the whiskers and everything." Dr. McMannequin took the phone out of my hand. Worked her way through a few more pictures. Appraising them with scrutiny. "Your ex-girlfriend was very pretty. Betcha regret fucking that one up, huh?"

"She broke up with me at SeaWorld. While we were on vacation," I said. "One minute we were watching the dolphin show and the next she was telling me she didn't find me attractive anymore. I was heartbroken. And I was crying like a little baby. And as she turned to walk away from me, she slipped on a banana peel and fell over the railing into the penguin enclosure. She survived the landing but those adorable little bastards tore her to shreds. By the time they were done she was nothing but a pile of bones and red smear on the ice."

"Love is certainly a fleeting thing," Dr. McMannequin said. "But you can't turn smoke back into a flame, Mr. Slater. Once the fire burns out, that's all she wrote."

"It was a very emotional time for me, as I'm sure you could imagine. But to their credit, the park manager recognized this and provided me with a voucher for a free corndog for my next visit. I never got to use this voucher but still, I appreciated the gesture."

The doctor zoomed in on the 2014 photo of me. Right at my hairline. Then once more inspected my scalp. "I guess I can kinda see the difference." She squinted. Held the phone up next to my head so she could compare the two side-by-side. I made the same face I was making in the picture. For verisimilitude.

"So whaddaya think, doc? Is there a way to salvage any of this? Or maybe grow it back?"

"I'm sorry but there is no growing it back, Mr. Slater. Male pattern baldness is unfortunately a one-way street."

"Right. While I understand that on an intellectual level, I thought this would all be a much slower process. Like, I know I'm 40 years old already and by no societal metric would I still be considered a 'young man' but I was always under the assumption that these kinds of changes would come on more gradually. Like the once-mighty mountain slowly eroding back into the Earth, I know that I too shall one day return to the dirt. Yet I can feel the hairs falling out as we speak. They are landing on the floor around us. It looks like a goddamn barbershop in here. Science and medicine were supposed to save me, were they not?"

Dr. McMannequin must have taken pity on me. She sat back down on her stool. Recrossed her legs. "I suppose it couldn't hurt to run a few tests. Make sure everything is functioning as it should. I mean, maybe you're right. Maybe this is symptomatic of something else. Maybe you have an issue with your *blenalia* that you don't know about yet."

"Yeah, that's probably it," I said. "It's probably just my *blenalia* acting up. But that ain't nothing that a few pills won't fix, right?"

"We'll find out soon enough." She wrote me a script and tore it loose from her pad. "But I want you to keep your expectations in check, Mr. Slater. Chances are, you've simply entered the next phase of your Gentleman's Journey, is all. And what you've been experiencing these past few weeks is just a perfectly natural expression of the aging process. You needn't fear the future, Mr. Slater. You should embrace it with both arms. Just ask my husband. He's as bald as a cue ball and I still fuck his brains out every night."

***

The blood lab was located in a strip mall on the outskirts of town. Sandwiched between an Applebee's and a T-Mobile store. I passed through a double set of doors into an ill-lit room full of weeping strangers. Music played. Brahms. I think. I had never actually heard Brahms before but I know he was one of those famous classical composer guys.

I pulled the tiny tab of paper from the red ticket-dispensing machine and sat there amid the rest of the sad-looking patients and waited for them to call my number. The process was not all that dissimilar to a supermarket deli. Here is a pint of most of my precious bodily fluids. Now give me a half-pound of Butterfield ham.

The phlebotomist called me back behind the pale blue curtain where they strapped me to the chair. People tend to wiggle too much, the phlebotomist said. I assured them I've never wiggled in my whole life but they told me it was protocol. They put some duct tape over my mouth.

My cabernet-colored blood flowed into the

HAIR PROBLEMS

vials. One after another. Until there were three. The phlebotomist slid the three vials into the centrifuge to their left and flipped a switch. The thing whirred to life. Spinning so fast I felt myself growing drowsy. As if I were hypnotized. I licked the backside of the tape until the adhesive weakened and the gag sloughed off.

"Hey, do you mind if I close my eyes for a bit and take a quick nap?" I asked them. "I couldn't sleep a wink last night. I've been worried sick about my encroaching baldness. It could be cancer. The doctor agreed. It's a distinct possibility, at least. I could have cancer right now and not even know it."

The phlebotomist nodded sympathetically. "Get some rest. I'll wake you in fifteen minutes or so. Your test results should be done by then."

So I dozed off in the chair and found myself amid a dreamless sleep. I don't dream like I did as a child. When I was little, I used to close my eyes and my imagination would take over. Paint vivid pictures in my head. Sometimes ameliorative. Sometimes nonsensical. Sometimes insightful. Sometimes terrifying. But they were always there. These dreams. As ever-present and indefatigable as the hair that once sat on my head.

But nowadays, when I close my eyes, I only have darkness to greet me on the other side. No more pictures in my head. No more promises to myself. Hope no longer splays out before me in these sprawling surreal narratives. There is real life and there is darkness and there is nothing in between.

When I woke up, I discovered the phlebotomist had already taken my blood out of the centrifuge and poured it into a few wine glasses and they and all the other people in the waiting room were having some kind of tasting. It seemed like a very classy affair, though as the phlebotomist took a sip and swished it around in their cheeks, a troubled expression washed across their face.

"What is this?" I asked. "Why is everyone drinking my blood? Is this how these things normally go? Is this Brahms you have playing over the loudspeaker? I am not nearly as cultured as I pretend to be on my Instagram posts. I've never been to the opera. I am only a marginally famous fiction writer. I've never had the kinds of experiences that would endow me with both a unique and relatable perspective, and as such, I will never ascend to the next phase in my writing career. I am boring, therefore my thoughts are boring."

The phlebotomist laid their hand on top of mine. Almost solemnly. "I think maybe you should have a word with the Big Nurse." They motioned to door in the back of the room with the words BIG NURSE stenciled across it. "She might be able to help give you some context as to what is going on."

I looked at the door and gulped. For some reason I felt like I was back in high school. Like I had gotten in trouble in class and was now being sent to the principal's office. I silently prayed that the Big Nurse was only calling me back there to have sex with me like the nurses often do in some of my favorite pornographic films. I'm specifically referencing *Night Nurses 7* which is widely considered by most critics as the apotheosis of the entire *Night Nurses* series. I told myself to remain calm. To not be too pushy. To let this situation play out naturally. If it happens, it happens, I said to myself. Just allow yourself to be open to the experience.

Turned out the Big Nurse was not interested in having sex with me. In fact, she looked even more troubled than the phlebotomist who sent me in here. I took a seat across from her as I tucked my penis back into my jockey shorts and rebuckled my belt.

The Big Nurse shuffled through the papers on her desk. "Mr. Slater, I called you in here because we've discovered a serious problem with your *blenalia*."

"I fuckin' knew it," I said. "So give it to me straight, nurse. Is it cancer? Is it chronic? Is my *hyper-blenalialism* the reason for all of my problems?"

"The problem is not *hyper-blenalialism*, Mr. Slater. The problem is that you have a *blenalia* in the first place."

"What do you mean?"

"Well as far as I know, the *blenalia* isn't a real organ."

"I'm sorry?"

"Anatomically-speaking, the *blenalia* doesn't exist. Not in humans. Not in animals. Not even plants. And from what I can gather, the word '*blenalia*' itself is completely made up."

"Well all words are made up, if you want to get technical about it."

Live Spooky, Die Spooky.

"You know what I mean, wise-ass. I'm saying there is no such thing as a *blenalia*."

"And yet, I apparently have this non-existent organ in my body?" I asked.

"Indeed you do," the Big Nurse replied. "And it's inflamed. Right there. Mid-abdomen. About a half-inch deep. Next to your *combannox* which, according to your bloodwork is also inflamed."

"My *combannox*?"

"Yes."

"What the hell is a *combannox*?"

"A *combannox* is also a non-existent organ. And you have one of those inside of you, too. In fact, from what these tests indicate, your entire body is completely filled with a wide array of nonsensical and non-existent organs. A *blenalia*. A *combannox*. A *dilingus mobo*. Both a lower and upper *gloopnaustagus*. None of these things are real, and yet, there they are, crowded up inside your chest like a bunch of teenagers in a mosh pit. Your blood isn't even blood. It's like some sort of molasses." She took a sip from the wine glass on her desk. "The flavor of it is hard to describe. There are smoky undertones to it with a fruity top note. Not completely unpleasant if it were to be paired with something like lamb or pasta."

"So are these strange organs and my syrupy blood responsible for my hair loss?" I asked.

"It honestly doesn't look like you're losing any hair from here," the Big Nurse replied.

"It's more about the density than the hairline itself," I told her. "If you were to scroll back through my Instagram feed, you'd be able to tell."

The Big Nurse nodded. "Well I don't want to be too hasty here. Diagnoses require due diligence. And while these superfluous body parts are certainly cause for concern, I couldn't say with 100% confidence that they are the root cause of your problem. We don't know what a *dilingus mobo* or a *gloopnaustagus* even do, let alone what might be wrong with them. Further testing will be needed if you want to know for sure. So I'm going to send you to an X-rayologist I know. He's very good. The best in the biz. He should be able to take a better look. Give you a more complete picture. And solve this mystery once and for all." The Big Nurse took another sip of my blood, chuckled, and shook her head. "Can you believe I initially called you back here to have sex with me?! Wild."

***

The radiology facility was located in the basement of an abandoned warehouse out near the old fishing wharves.

The X-rayologist was a tall skinny man who welcomed me down the concrete staircase with all the theatrical flair of a circus barker. Into the dark chamber of his examination room I was ushered.

He wore a devilish smile on his face the entire time. And for a moment, I thought he was going to try to have sex with me too, like some of the men in my *other* favorite pornographic series *Construction Site Cum Daddies*. Yeah, it's a long shot but after things failed to materialize romantically with the Big Nurse I was feeling very vulnerable. While I refused to allow myself to get too worked up—I was here for a medical procedure, after all—I tried to remain open to the possibility that love might find me in the end. Who knows? Maybe the X-rayologist and I were meant to be together. Maybe he would move in with me and we would carve a pumpkin in the shape of my cat. Maybe, one day, I will heal enough to be able to return to SeaWorld. And I will finally get my free corndog. And I won't let the penguins take the X-rayologist from me. Not this time.

"Please lie in my cozy little machine here." The lanky technician motioned to a box in the middle of the room, the exact same size and shape as a coffin. "It's state-of-the-art and perfectly safe," he assured me. "I will lock it from the outside to make sure nobody can get in."

The box was lined with satin. Really quite classy. And very soft. I appreciated the X-rayologist's concern for my comfort. It was one of his most endearing qualities. I had to do an MRI once. It was really loud. Not like in this coffin. No sir. In this coffin, things felt serene and secure. I very much appreciated this X-rayologist's methodology and commitment to professionalism.

Click. The deadbolt latched into place.

Honk. What I imagined to be some kind of big red button being pressed.

Zap. X-rays bombarded my body from every direction at once.

Bing. The bell above the door of the office chimed as someone else entered the facility. Some kind of heavy-footed man. Through the lid of the

HAIR PROBLEMS

coffin I could hear the sounds of a scuffle. And the X-rayologist shouting.

"What are you doing, barging in like this? Can't you see I'm already with a patient? You need to wear a lead vest to protect yourself from the harmful radiation. Put on this special underwear if you're going to come in here. And then dance. Dance for me. Wait, what is that in your hand? A hunting knife? What are you planning to do with that?"

"What's happening?" I cried out. "Who is here? What do they want?"

"It's some kind of man with what I could only describe as a tweaker-hungry look in his eye," the X-rayologist said. "He says he knows you. He says you two met before. He says you made him feel emasculated when he tried to carjack you and you just drove away. You were supposed to be afraid of him, he says. And when you refused to cower in fear, you broke the social contract. He says he's felt unmoored since then. He says he is full of ennui. He says he would do anything to get things back to the way they once were. The way they were supposed to be. He says ever since that fateful day he's been following you. Weeks. Months. However long it's been. He says time is relative. He says the days feel long and the years feel short. He says we only have so much time before we shuffle off this mortal coil and once we do, we are gone forever. He says there is no Heaven and no Hell. No place of understanding or peace or oneness. He says there is only nothingness. He says we are all destined for the void. He says he's been watching your every move. He knows when you eat. He knows when you sleep. Your beloved cat that you let sit in your lap when you watch TV? Well he wants you to know that that's been him in a fur suit this whole time."

These revelations were off-putting, to say the least. I felt violated. I felt confused. I had tried very hard to get to the bottom of my hair loss, and in the interim, things had only gotten worse. And I thought, perhaps Dr. McMannequin was right. Perhaps this was the kind of problem with no solution. Perhaps I could just embrace my future as a cue ball.

But instead a fire grew within me, in the very pit of my soul, if you believe in such things. Small, at first. Just a flicker in the darkness. But it was enough. Rome was once the capital of the world until it burned to the ground. Every conflagration began with a single spark.

I cried out to the X-rayologist from inside my box. "Can you tell my would-be carjacker that while I am duly impressed by his commitment, I will not apologize for standing up for myself. I will not allow the world to victimize me."

The X-rayologist began to repeat the things I just said, but was cut off when the carjacker decided to stab him. I could hear him gurgling on his own blood as the knife went in and out of his face 453 times. And he died.

The padlock on the coffin held firm, even as I continued to pound against it. The satin was so soft it absorbed all the urgency out of my blows. To the carjacker it sounded like I was merely tapping. Tap tap tap. As lightly as the breeze.

"Let me out of here!" I screamed. "Let me out! Please! I'm sorry I didn't let you steal my car! I'm sorry that I didn't react the way I was supposed to! You can have my car now! You can be my cat too! Whatever you want! Whatever you need! I just don't want to die! Please!"

And the x-rays continued to pummel me. Beams of radiation played my bones like I were a xylophone. My insides rumbled. I was being boiled alive. Molasses-thick blood bubbled up, alongside my liquefied organs. My *blenalia*. My *combannox*. My *dilingus mobo*. Both my lower and upper *gloopnaustagus*. The whole of me now reduced to a thick hot sludge. Leaking out of my nose. Leaking out of all of my orifices. Soaking into the expensive fabric that surrounded me. Ruining the satin. I would probably be charged to replace it.

This was my final resting place. This was my unavoidable fate. From the very moment I saw the first hair fall from my head, this was always going to be the unceremonious end to my Gentleman's Journey. I realize that now.

But just because certain things are inevitable doesn't mean I have to be happy about it, does it?

And with that thought, there it was. My anger. Still within me. Hibernating all this time. And now it was awake. Now I could feel it, blossoming, billowing, surging through my veins. As fresh and as raw as I remembered it. Righteous anger. Wonderful anger. Cleansing anger. Cathartic anger. The only goggles through which I can see

Live Spooky, Die Spooky.

DANGER SLATER

the truth. I vowed right then and there I would never abandon my anger again. And as I hammered my fists against the lid of my coffin and screamed and thrashed in futile rage, it felt like I was finally coming home.

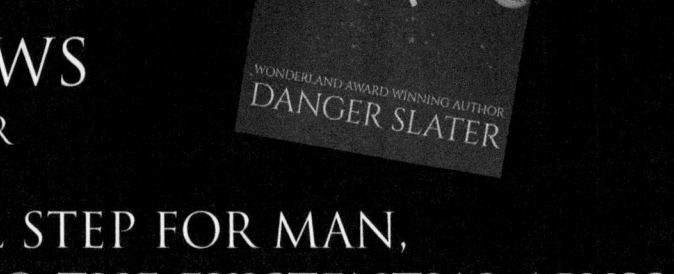

MOONFELLOWS
BY DANGER SLATER

ONE SMALL STEP FOR MAN,
ONE GIANT LEAP INTO THE EXISTENTIAL ABYSS

WWW.GHOULISH.RIP

ALSO BY DANGER SLATER

STARLET

COMING SOON!

WWW.GHOULISH.RIP

THE ACT ONE DOG
Animals & Horror

E. F. Schraeder

I'M FINALLY ALL set up to watch the latest horror movie everyone is raving about, and by the end of the credits I'm hooked, enjoying the hell out of the vibe. Right up until the dog bounces onscreen, tail wagging.

The Act One Dog. Yep, I know what's going to happen. Will I be watching? Nope.

Whether I'm streaming at home or sitting in a theater, I'll either skip ahead or dart out for popcorn in about thirteen to seventeen minutes. Why? Because violence toward animals is uncomfortable as fuck to witness for a lot of reasons, even when it's fake. Honestly, even Betty Rocksteady's Ghoulish nod to the infamous Cheeseface cover is a teeny bit wince-inducing because of the familiar visual association it prompts.

I'll avoid the inevitable animal's fate, mostly because it's nothing like the fun adrenaline rush I associate with the pleasant thrills of movie-viewing fear. It's what happens in the animal's next act that I want to avoid because it's oh-so-tragic (and also oh-so-predictable). The Act One Dog is as common a trope as The Final Girl, but unlike her the Act One Dog rarely makes it out alive.

But first, let's indulge in considering a variety of Act One Dogs and for context, note the Act One Dog appears in multiple genres. A handful of examples off the top of my head takes literally zero effort. Just think about how things go for the animals: action fans have *John Dies at the End* (2012), *John Wick* (2014); comedy lovers *National Lampoon's Vacation* (1983), *There's Something About Mary* (1998), *The Royal Tenenbaums* (2001); romance offers *Marley & Me* (2008); drama delivers *Of Mice and Men* (1939) and *Let Him Go* (2020); thrillers like *Rear Window* (1954) and *Fatal Attraction* (1987) don't flinch; even family films like *Bambi* (1942), *Old Yeller* (1957), *All Dogs Go to Heaven* (1989), *My Dog Skip* (2000) play along; and we can't forget science fiction classics like *The Fly II* (1989) and *Hollow Man* (2000). I'm not even going to touch apocalypse films. So many viewers abhor the trend of animal cruelty and death in films that there's an online database dedicated to answering one and only one plot question: Does The Dog Die?

Every genre seems to offer useful animal-emo tropes, and in horror the set list also grows impossibly long with minimal effort. Seriously, think of a horror film with an animal and it's probably an animal that dies. Early. Whether it's a quick emotional hook or a sucker punch, sometimes the animal isn't a dog like the cat in *Count Yorga, Vampire* (1970), the horse in *The Ring* (2002), or a bird *Poltergeist* (1982), *Hereditary* (2018). Any innocent creature will do. These animals serve a particular purpose, maybe symbolizing vulnerability, providing easy access to empathy, or setting up discomfort. One of the most popular screenwriting manuals in a decade is named *Save the Cat*, after all.

As Carol Clover pointed out in her landmark book *Men, Women and Chainsaws* (1992), target-making in horror often placed women in the crosshairs of whatever malignant evils lurk in the film, whether supernatural or ordinary. But with the First Act Dog we get a precursor: animals serve as a set up. For horror-goers, the Second Act Flip helps writers make good on that ready-made pang animal-induced anxiety. It's in The Flip stage of horror films that viewers identify who the human targets will be for the duration of the film. The Flip swaps viewers' feelings and concerns for the nonhuman animal with the protagonist, the vulnerable human who becomes the target of evil. The Flip is clear across sub-genres: in monster movies like *The Curse of Frankenstein* (1957) and *Ginger Snaps* (2000); supernatural features like The *Amityville Horror* (1979) and *The Babadook* (2014); unstoppable slashers like *Halloween* (1978), *A Nightmare on Elm Street* (2010), or the rant about person-as-meat in *Scream* (2022). The human-as-animal Flip functions whether the film attempts an empathic, antagonistic, or sympathetic lens.

The Flip makes a bold jump, evoking an emotional response to human life initially prompted by the fate of the Act One Dog. Perhaps the more viewers were shocked and frightened for the animal, the harder they root for the substituted protagonist(s). Once the human is subjected to the terrible threats that already defeated the Act One Dog, this exposes the underlying horrors of devalued animal life. Whatever the motive, the Flip effectively inverts the moral status quo that assigns high value to human life by equating human and animal death.

Ultimately, human victims assume center stage and emotive viewer reactions are achieved with the use of this topsy-turvy moral inversion. It bears noting that these substitutions involve a degree of objectification, relying on a comparison drawn out by Carol J. Adams in the iconic *The Sexual Politics of Meat* (1990) and later work, where people identified as 'women' become absent referents, not subjects but objects regarded as animals. From Adams' view, animals are constructed and viewed in feminized ways, subjugated and valued mostly for their parts and pieces. They are used to satisfy the cravings of the powerful, victims both human and animal are churned out for the reaction. In horror, the comparison widens to an objectified view of victims, all of whom are in some sense, 'animalized.' The Flip is effective because the unconscious association operates seamlessly—a functional centerpiece in the horror genre where both Clover's and Adams' premises are at work and entwined.

The conflicts and triumphs of course vary, but in the end, Act Three provides a Moral Wrap, with either a full return to the pre-existing status quo or a total inversion of moral expectations and continued threat (often in the shape of a sequel franchise). Either human dominion and order over the natural world emerges, restored, or the world enters full submersion into moral chaos.

Either way, human dominance over animal life dictates the terms of the morality and the horror. As Barry Keith Grant points out in the classic *The Dread of Difference: Gender and the Horror Film* (2015), horror depends on and is defined by transgressive treatments of norms. Extending these theoretical understandings beyond the lens of gender and into the realm of species provides another way to recognize uncomfortable truths about humanity's relationship to the natural world and other animals on earth. As I write, casual estimates assume that human exploitation of natural resources is at least in part responsible for climate change and nearly one million species facing the brink of extinction. Maybe the primal angst I feel when I see a dog onscreen in a horror movie is because even seated in my comfortable movie-viewing chair I know how brutal the real world is for animals—and for all of us.

Let's return briefly to that infamous dog on the cover Cheeseface, and the influential magazine. Maybe the image changed humor in the U.S., but was it really all that transgressive? In real life, the Vermont dog was shot and killed. In Vermont and probably elsewhere, there were lots of dogs shot that year (1976). To be groundbreaking, wouldn't it be more interesting to subvert a norm? Interrupt a dominant perspective? Or at least reveal a troublesome trend? Is it fair to call something shocking if practically everyone knows what's next?

Horror cinema bursts with reflections of deep seated fears, things most folks would prefer to forget about. These bloody movies reflect the bloody awful things people do in the real world. This three-act lens may help me better understand terror and as a horror enthusiast, I'm interested in untwisting those layers of fear. Amidst the

THE ACT ONE DOG: ANIMALS & HORROR

complications in horror, I find some simple insights about what we humans seem to fear most: being killed, being eaten, being tortured. In short, the horror of being viewed and treated as (gasp) the animals we are.

Everyone knows the woman who escapes a massacre is a final girl, but who is the final boy? *What Happened Was Impossible* follows the life of Ida Wright, a man who knows how to capitalize on his childhood tragedies . . . even when he caused them.

Order Now!
www.GhoulishBooks.com

Live Spooky, Die Spooky.

LUCY WEST IS NOT A STAGE NAME

Jennifer Elise Wang

I MET LUCY WEST while tasked with picking up her underwear. I was a stage kitten, burlesque's version of a stagehand—more visible, less clothed. Without the stilettos and headdress, she was a small woman (even compared to my 5'3" self). Nevertheless I felt like I was approaching a larger-than-life entity—a goddess—when I had to ask her about any props she needed me to set up. She was an international burlesque star and headliner of our show for a reason.

I stood a couple feet away from her makeup table, shifting uncomfortably and hoping my thong was not riding up my ass crack. Lucy had been giggling with the performer next to her, and I didn't want to interrupt their conversation.

"I was briefly a Betty too, Betty Bloofer! How silly of a name was that? I thought it was cute, and while it worked for vaudeville . . ." She stopped and made eye contact with me through the mirror. "You can come closer, honey. I don't bite."

Her smile somehow made me not believe her, but I had a job to do. Lucy, however, seemed determined to keep me for herself. Thankfully there was another stage kitten, but I glanced at the other performers to make sure I wasn't getting the side eye. I don't think they dared to counter the wishes of a performer like Lucy.

Although she was still idly doing her makeup, the redhead looked stage ready. Maybe she was quick at applying most of her makeup. She had a sharp jawline and high cheekbones that a Kardashian would envy, a thin nose, and incredibly plump red lips. Long lashes framed those cool blue eyes, and her porcelain skin had not a single blemish or wrinkle. On the other hand, I was already developing frown lines at nineteen. "Tell me your name, darling," she said.

"Vic—Mina Mori." I was still getting used to introducing myself by my stage name.

"Mina . . ."

"Yeah, *Bram Stoker's Dracula* is my favorite movie, and I just think Winona Ryder is so cool. And Mori can mean 'death' or 'forest' depending on the language and my last name means 'forest' in Chinese even though it's a different character than what 'mori' is in Japanese."

Lucy smiled at my rambling, which made me more anxious. So I kept talking, "Have you seen the Coppola version of *Dracula*? It's a lot closer to the book than other movies, but it's still different. More romantic and sexy."

Her smile widened to a toothy grin. Even her teeth were immaculate. "It's always interesting how each interpretation differs." She paused before adding, "You don't have to be so nervous around me. Like I said, I don't bite . . . at least not fellow performers . . . without their consent."

"Sorry, I'm still pretty new to this—and, like, you're Lucy West! You came here from England! I never thought I'd be in a show with you."

She laughed. "Ah, to be so young like you again! I've lived in the States before, Texas actually. I even performed in the Carousel Club."

It was my turn to smile since I could show off my knowledge of burlesque history. "Didn't Dallas have a show named after Jack Ruby's nightclub? I know that club doesn't exist anymore, but it's cool that they're still paying homage to it and Tammi True was at the Dallas Burlesque Festival a few years ago."

I didn't get to hear Lucy's response because Candela Rouge, the other stage kitten, appeared between us. "Kirsten wants us to help her set up the merch table," she said bluntly.

I turned to follow Candela and felt long pointed fingernails graze my wrist. I looked back. "It was nice talking with you, *Mina*."

Lucy said my name with something akin to familiarity or fondness. I hoped that she really meant we could be in another show together. Or at the very least, be willing to talk to me again.

***

Candela and I were hustling for the rest of the evening until the final act, which was Lucy's second number of the evening and her signature act. Normally cast and crew could only get tiny glimpses of the performer on-stage through cracks in the curtain, but we all shuffled into a dark corner by the backstage entrance to see Lucy. She came out in a white gown with a giant lace collar—it reminded me of an Elizabethan ruff but more opulent and less stifling—and a white, rhinestone-covered headdress dripping in scarlet beads. "Night Train" was pretty much a burlesque cliché, but Lucy owned the jazz standard, flirting with the front row and then pulling back as if bashful.

Midway through the piece, she tore off the gown and revealed ruby red lingerie that matched the beading of her headdress. The music changed, and even though I knew the soft beginning was a deceptive start to Otep's "Ghost Flowers", I remained unprepared for the ferocity with which Lucy began to dance. Gone was the coquette and in her place was a lioness on the prowl, reaching out with those pointed fingernails and smacking her Pleaser heels to the floor as she dropped to her knees. Suddenly I understood what people meant when they said, "Step on me". Her collar had concealed Isis wings that made her even more imposing. Most dancers looked like butterflies with the prop, but she reminded me of an owl ready to swoop down at us mice.

When Lucy had stripped to her teardrop-shaped pasties and G-string, our producer Kirsten Kizmet shooed Candela and me back through the door so we could get ready to pick up the discarded costume pieces. The spell was broken for us at least, and the other performers followed us to prepare for curtain call. There still wasn't any time to say anything to Lucy besides, "Where should I put your gown?" so I wasn't sure whether my earlier awkwardness had put her off.

Finally we all took our bows, and it was time to mingle with the audience and promote the next show. I lurked around the corner I had been watching Lucy perform, as fans and friends of the performers chatted them up. Candela went to get a drink with her partner, leaving me alone and wondering whether I should just pack my things up, get paid, and head out.

"It was nice to see you again, Mimi," I heard someone say. "Now when will it be your turn to perform?"

A balding older man in a pinstripe suit sidled up next to me—a little too close. I'd seen him at some previous shows and others around town but managed to avoid him until now. While most super fans are just really enthusiastic about burlesque like I was before I decided to perform, I vaguely remember someone saying this man was a creep. Nevertheless I didn't want to be rude, especially in case I had the wrong guy or the rumor was false. "I'm just starting, and actually my name is Mina."

"Where can I see you perform?"

I shrugged. "I submitted to a couple shows but nothing confirmed yet."

"You should perform here. You're beautiful, Minnie."

"Well, it takes more than just looks." I tried to make my laugh more playful than nervous, but I wasn't sure how convincing I was, especially with my eyes darting around for a familiar and available face to run to.

"You look so young." Unlike with Lucy, I really didn't like the way he honed in on my age. "Are you in school? Or do you work in the day?"

"I—" I wanted to tell him that my personal life was none of his business, but directness was never my forte.

"Oh Mina, there you are." Lucy appeared so suddenly that I jumped. "I still need a picture with you."

The man seemed equally startled, even intimidated. Lucy was still in her lingerie, headdress, and heels so she loomed over us. As she bent to put her face next to mine for a selfie, she whispered, "There's an after-party at Las Palapas. You should go."

I wasn't sure if she meant for me to take the out or that I should join the after-party, which she may even not be attending, but her suggestion felt more like a command. Her voice was not stern, yet I felt a force in my chest that made me want to obey without hesitation. Even though a veteran like Lucy probably knew how to deal with creepers, I didn't want to ditch her. But my feet were already carrying me back to the dressing room, as I heard her tell the man, "I'm so delighted to find someone who recognized 'Hard Hearted Hannah!'"

***

I hung around the dressing room as everyone else packed up, pretending to make sure everything was clean. In reality, I was hoping to catch Lucy again. Her stuff was still on her makeup table, and it was just Kirsten and me left. "Thank you for helping clean up, but I think we're done. Except Lucy. I'm not sure where she went." The producer sighed. "I'll go find her. Do you need me to get you an escort to your car?"

"It's okay, I didn't park too far."

"Be careful. You gonna get tacos with us?"

"For a little bit. See you there."

As I told Kirsten, I parked close to the theatre, so I thought nothing of the solitary walk to my car. Still the backside of the theatre really showed its age and the poor lighting added to the eerie mood. Tonight in particular, an uneasy feeling came over me. Maybe it was the lingering social anxiety from my interactions with Lucy. Maybe it was the effects of receiving my first burlesque creeper interaction. A shiver ran through me even though I had changed back into my T-shirt and jeans, which it was too hot for in July even at night.

Suddenly I heard a muffled sound near the dumpster. Perhaps a little foolishly, I headed towards it instead of my car. I was a sucker for rescuing stray cats. I took my pepper spray out of my purse, just in case.

A flash of red disappeared around the unused side building. Most people stayed away from that aging part of the theatre. I should have done the same, but something beyond just a need to save a potential kitten in need kept me going.

Before I could re-think my decision, somethingme against the brick wall, one familiar manicured hand at my throat and another around my hand with the pepper spray. It was Lucy, still half-naked but now with maroon smeared down her chin and between her breasts.

"Oh my dear, sweet Mina. You seemed to have rushed my plans." There was that unsettling grin again, but now I could see the extended canines.

I didn't want to look to the side, but I could see a striped pant leg in my periphery. "I—You—him . . ."

"Use your words, my dear. Use your head, Mina."

What did she mean by that? The claw-like fingernails at my throat started to stroke my chin. I didn't know if I was being hypnotized or impossibly attracted to her, but I became calm enough to study that pale, marble-smooth face—too smooth. Too pale before she put the bronzer on while we talked. Carousel Club. Dracula interpretations. Betty *Bloofer*. "Lucy West," I said aloud.

"Yes?"

"Lucy West is not a stage name. Lucy West-en-ra," I finished. "But you didn't die?"

"I found it more advantageous to let Mr. Stoker alter the events so my Mina and I could continue our travels."

"So he knew?"

"While he was alive."

I recalled learning that different sources listed different causes for Bram Stoker's death. None of them mentioned a blood disease or foul play, but I supposed if nobody in my life believed in vampires and I was staring at one right now, they must have been good at concealing their existence. "Will you kill me too to keep your secret?" I asked.

She laughed. "I could, but I had different plans for you. Of course, I was going to wait until you let me become your burly mama, but it seems fate wanted to speed things up. You see, my Mina grew tired of this un-life even when I let her have Jonathan by her side for eternity."

"You want me to be her replacement?"

Lucy let go of me to start wiping the blood off her face with the back of her hand. The gesture seemed so human to me that I dug a tissue out of my purse. "Thank you, darling. And no, nothing will replace my Mina. But I have grown tired of superficial relationships, and you cannot deny that how uncanny our meeting has been."

Her playful façade gave way to earnestness. "Listen, you can continue to do burlesque and keep whatever friends and family you have for a brief period, but there will be many lies and a time when you have to cut things off. On top of this." She held up the bloody tissue, grinning again.

I hadn't believed in fate, but far too many coincidences lined up to make this the perfect scenario for Lucy: my stage name, my love of *Dracula*, my idolization of her, moving to San Antonio on my own. My phone dinged, and I remembered Kirsten was still looking for her headliner. Lucy must have realized the same because she was pressing up against me again, lips at my throat. "Time's up, my dear. I am going to bite you either way, but you will decide whether things end there or not."

We never did make it to the after-party.

THE ONLY SAFE PLACE LEFT IS THE DARK

BY WARREN WAGNER

www.Ghoulish.rip

AN HIV POSITIVE GAY MAN MUST LEAVE THE RELATIVE SAFETY OF HIS CABIN IN THE WOODS TO BRAVE THE ZOMBIE APOCALYPSE AND FIND THE MEDICATION HE NEEDS TO STAY ALIVE.

THE SKIN OF REEMA LAL

Saswati Chatterjee

1

The skin of Reema Lal followed her killer home.

It wrapped around his foot as he slept and sank in, only skin deep. The sleeping man would have felt nothing, perhaps an itch. He would have swatted at it, like one swats at a mosquito. The skin smoothened itself, settling over folds and body hair like it belonged there.

The next morning, the leg was stiff and cold, beginning to turn purple. The doctor scratched his head, called it gangrene and pronounced that the limb would have to be amputated.

And so the skin gained a leg.

Hindu rituals call for bodies to be cremated; hospital protocols need body parts to be incinerated as biohazards. Either way, it was meant for the fire. But the skin wrapped itself around the neck of the orderly meant to take away the limb, forcing him to run for the nearest bathroom to vomit as it reclaimed the leg and simply hopped away. The halls of Netaji Subhash Chandra Bose District Hospital are still haunted by tales of a single hopping leg.

What is a single leg to a body? As Mohan Lal lay recovering at home, his thoughts went to a phantom itch in his now missing leg. He dreamt of scratching it vigorously, of being rid of the unceasing itch now only in his mind. The skin, now a leg, returned at night and gently reattached itself to its former owner's body. And as Mohan Lal put a hand down to scratch that long-neglected itch, the skin wrapped around his arm.

The scream that followed set the neighborhood dogs to howling.

***

The doctors at Netaji Subhash Chandra Bose District Hospital were, to put it in a word, flabbergasted. Mohan Lal lay before them, one arm as pale as the sheet he lay on. The first doctor who had examined him could not find a vein in the arm at first. Then when he did, there was no blood that drew into the syringe. All this while Mohal Lal lay on the bed and moaned and ranted to the skies about *that bitch—that whore—*

He was referred to a blood specialist. There was none in their tiny government hospital in Gorakhpur so a special ambulance was arranged to carry their patient to Lucknow, and from there to New Delhi. There, he was taken to the All India Institute of Medical Sciences where a battalion of doctors came down to look at the single white limb that lay starkly attached to its owner's body.

And so the skin bided its time.

***

Mohan Lal was sure he was dying. Every night, that wretched dream visited him, where his phantom leg itched and his arm, his useless right arm, filled with blood and swelled as if it had become a giant mosquito, heavy with drink. He itched and swore and cursed. He wanted to prick the giant mosquito, bleed it out. He closed his eyes and called for nurses and cursed *that bitch, that whore—*

The skin had been at the hospital for a week now and it had had plenty of time to do whatever it liked. It had learned the hospital's layout,

THE SKIN OF REEMA LAL

wrapping softly and carefully around the arms of nurses and orderlies as they walked the corridors and floors of the building. It had watched as doctors and nurses drifted in and out of the patient's room, some working, some consulting, some gawping. All coming to look at the man with a missing leg and an arm as white as snow.

By now his story had reached newspapers and a few journalists had reached out to the hospital, asking about the strange new patient. None of them managed to get in to see the man himself, though plenty of speculative reports were written.

AIIMS Tight Lipped About New Patient. Is This The Start Of A New Disease?

"I Don't Know Anything": Watch An AIIMS Doctor Respond When Asked Questions About New Disease!

Medical Industry Closes Ranks Over New Disease

And still the skin bided its time.

***

On the eve of Mohan Lal's second week at AIIMS, Dr. Arbaaz, the chief supervising physician, told him that they were sending him to the United States. They were at their wits' end here, he explained, and doctors at Johns Hopkins Medicine had expressed interest. But not to worry, he reassured, Mohan Lal wasn't going to go alone. Two doctors from AIIMs would personally accompany him there.

If Mohan Lal was reassured, he was incapable of showing it. His moans and rants had given way to an almost stupefied silence. Nurses said he barely slept. If asked, he said little, scratched the empty air below the left side of his hip and muttered about dreams. Through it all, he barely acknowledged the lifeless arm next to him.

The nurses talked among themselves. He, they said, slept in the day, with his eyes roaming beneath closed lids, *yes just like he did now, Didi did you see it?* At night, he lay awake, clutching his arm and shaking. Occasionally he would weep.

And when he was sure no nurse was watching, he would whisper, half-savage, half terrified, *Kahan hai tu? Kahan hai tu?*

Where are you?

And when silence greeted his words, he would moan and rock back and forth on his hospital cot as the skin waited and watched.

***

There was an airplane waiting to take him to America. Mohan Lal had never been on one before; even the trip from Gorakhpur to New Delhi had been by train (from Gorakhpur to Lucknow and then an express straight to the capital). The doctor who had come to tell him the news was beaming; clearly, he thought, this was news that would cheer Mohan Lal up. On his part, the star patient was quiet and guarded, apparently listening as the doctor described to him the facilities, the sights and smells of America that he was to expect. As he stopped to draw breath, Mohan Lal asked if he was going to be taken to a skin specialist.

The doctor looked at him, astonished. No, he said. Well, they were going to many specialists, and skin certainly might be among them, but considering the state of his arm and the lack of *blood*, they would be going to a hematologist first, a blood specialist, you know—

"*Nahin,*" Mohan Lal answered gloomily. "*Aap galat soch rahe hain. Ye khoon ka mamla nahin hai.*"

You're wrong. This isn't a matter of blood.

He proved unforthcoming after that, no matter the line of questioning. Medical tests had dried up in terms of results and the patient himself was no longer able, or willing, to answer any more questions. Two surgeons were selected, esteemed representatives of their respective departments, and it was agreed that Mohan Lal was to be flown the next day.

That night, the leg hopped quietly to the bed and inserted itself back into its former position. The skin slid off and slithered up the dead white arm until it was at the neck. It felt the Adam's apple bob underneath and wrapped itself ever so lovingly around the throat of the man who had killed Reema Lal.

Mohan Lal awoke to an agony of terror and felt for his throat. In this he failed, as one arm lay dead and unmoving to his right while the other shuddered in its position, mind and muscle unable to resist a pull that held it flat against the cold metal railing of the cot. Mohan Lal opened his lips—to call for the nurse, to pray to the gods—and the skin slithered inside.

Live Spooky, Die Spooky.

SASWATI CHATTERJEE

2

It was Nurse Rani who found her first. On that day, she was the earliest to reach ward number sixty-three. That was only natural for her; as head nurse, she was there in her official capacity to check on their patient before the chief physician arrived to supervise his move from hospital to airport, and in her unofficial capacity to keep any busybodies or curious nurses from bothering their infamous patient.

The night nurse was packing up as she arrived; they exchanged brief reports before the woman left, tired eyes indicating a long night. Nurse Rani changed into her uniform, transforming into her brisk, no-nonsense self, before heading into the ward. She already had her day planned in her head—an endless list of tasks to get through after checking on Mohan Lal.

The only occupied bed was at the end of the ward. When the nurse walked over, she saw that the girl was just sitting there, almost motionless. Her arms were wrapped around her thin legs, which were brought up against her chest. Her hair was cleanly brushed and plaited, almost like a schoolgirl's. Her hands were small and ended in bitten nails. Her eyes, when they met the nurse's, were small and bright. She smiled from where she sat on Mohan Lal's bed.

Its actual occupant was nowhere to be seen.

***

In later remembrance, most of the nurses of AIIMS would remember *this* part of the 'incident' (as it came to be called) with some confusion; nobody could exactly recall what had happened in what order. Certainly at some point, Dr. Arbaaz was roused by a distraught Nurse Rani, who informed him that his star patient could not be found. Before his hurried arrival, nurses and doctors alike had scattered throughout the hospital, in desperate search of a man who, before this day, had not been able to move from his bed.

Somebody floated the idea of murder, which then spread through the hospital like wildfire until eventually it reached the ears of the police, who then brought dogs to sniff through the ground of the hospital in hopes of turning up some unfortunate body.

They found nothing, of course. No bodies, nor any signs of a murder. It was suggested by the police that the man had simply left; maybe he had had enough of being treated as a scientific specimen. This suggestion seemed to engender some resentment among the doctors.

But that too fell through. No guards had spotted him leaving; the night nurse swore up and down that he had never left the room while she was there. The CCTV cameras backed up their claims: there was no sign of this man ever leaving his room, never mind the hospital. It was like he had disappeared without a trace.

No, not without a trace. There was the girl, of course.

She looked to be no older than ten or eleven. Quiet and eerily self-possessed, she had little or no answers for the frustrated officers questioning her. She had no guardian, no apparent knowledge of how she came to the hospital. She could not name a single person in the hospital that she knew. Only one thing she answered, almost thoughtfully, to a more sympathetic nurse: her name, spoken through bites of a chocolate bar.

"Reema."

And that was it. No last name could be coaxed from her. She almost seemed amused by the efforts to get answers out of her; as if she was the puzzle, rather than their missing patient. Which she was; much like the case of the man's disappearance, there was the matter of her *appearance*. The CCTVs had caught no signs of a little girl walking in. The nurses had never seen her, no guard recognised her. It was impossible to think that she, like some intrepid reporters, had scaled the walls of the hospital, and even if she *had*, for what reason?

There were no answers and therefore, in the absence of the truth, they settled for lies.

"Patient ran away," they reported to the eager salivating newspapers waiting at the doorsteps of the hospital. They left out any mention of the girl (some truths are too strange to cover up with lies) and the Head of the Hematology Department at All India Medical Institute, New Delhi sent an apologetic email to his counterpart in John Hopkins Medicine. He hastened to add that, undoubtedly, there had been very little wrong with the man in question anyway, including a last

THE SKIN OF REEMA LAL

conciliatory line about hoping for a further chance at collaboration.

With the last of the 't's crossed and the 'i's dotted, there was simply the question of what to do with the girl.

In actuality, there was little to do but hand her over to the police. With nothing more than a name and no traceable family, it was the right (and most convenient) option. A Child Welfare Officer was assigned to pick her up. With this, she could now simply cease to be a problem of the hospital, who wanted to close this frankly embarrassing chapter and be done with it.

It wasn't until all this was decided that someone thought to come and talk to Reema herself about it. All through the hullabaloo, she had been housed at a kind nurse's home (the one who had offered her chocolate) and it was she who broke the news to her as gently as possible.

"They are nice people," the nurse said to the child, hoping against hope that it was true. "They'll find you a safe place to stay. You'll be happier there." Absently, she wiped biscuit crumbs from the corners of the girl's mouth.

"Okay," said Reema, with apparent unconcern about her fate. "Do I have to go now?" She took a big bite from another biscuit.

"Not immediately," the nurse said, frowning at the girl as she brushed off more crumbs. For a moment, she was sure something was off in the image of the placid, serene girl sitting in front of her. But she couldn't put a finger on it.

Reema looked at her, and the nurse felt as if she was being seen for the first time.

"What happened to the man?"

This was the first time she had shown interest, or any kind of acknowledgement, of the 'incident'.

"Which man?"

"The man in the bed."

The nurse hesitated. "We don't know," she said finally. When the eyes remained fixed on her, she relented and added, "With an arm like that? He's probably dead somewhere."

Was she dreaming, or did those eyes widen? Widen, until the skin was limber and loose beneath them, as it folded upon folds that should not exist. Reema was smiling at her, and the smile rippled through her skin, which creased up in seams—all smiles of their own—and then went taut again, a child's skin.

"Is that so?"

"Yes." The nurse's own skin was suddenly very tight and cold. "Yes . . . he's dead."

Reema Lal smiled again, skin creasing naturally, like paper. "Good."

Live Spooky, Die Spooky.

JUDE DOE

perfect kiss strickoll

JUDE DIES ON the property five times and the first time he is already dying when the man who owns the motel finds him under the NO VACANCY sign, bleeding out. "Shot," he gurgles as he dies, and then that's it, he's dead. All that moves is the blood that seeps from his stomach into the grass, impossible in the night's dark, all motion and no color. The man who owns the motel calls the paramedics and they come with the slow ambulance, no lights. They come with a body bag. The whole ordeal is like a dream to the man who owns the motel, and the next morning he could believe that it really was if not for the red smear in the grass under the NO VACANCY sign, if not for the fact that it is New Year's Day, 1960, for the second time.

That night it storms like the dickens and the roads are quiet, and the man who owns the motel sits in the office with a cup of hot coffee and a record on. He doesn't look up when the door creaks open because sometimes he sees and hears things—things like small bursts of beautiful blue light and things like the voice of his father, long dead. But when he feels wind blow rain onto his skin he looks up and standing there is the man who died under the NO VACANCY sign last night, which is also tonight. His name is Jude.

In the light Jude is the most beautiful thing the man who owns the motel has ever seen, and the trade he deals in delivers all sorts of beautiful things to the office: loose women and wayward queers. Fake blonde and young, five years different from the man who owns the motel, maybe a decade. The kind of would-be-customer the man who owns the motel's father would have exercised his right to refuse service to, years ago, when *he* was the man who owned the motel. Jude is wearing cut-offs and a button-up shirt so white that in the storm he might as well not be wearing it. When he walks up to the counter it's with a swing to his hips that lets the man who owns the motel know that *he* knows all of these observations are true, that he is a beautiful thing even soaked from the rain, even dying under the NO VACANCY sign.

Jude is so beautiful that when he says two things, that his name is Jude and that he doesn't have any money, the man who owns the motel is already poisoned. What you need to understand is that there is not yet any cultural script for how this kind of thing goes, no golden age of pornography. Jude knows how it goes and the man who owns the motel does not. All he knows is the wicked intimacy between two men that he has never experienced, and the wicked hotness that starts to broil in his stomach when Jude looks at him like that, talks to him like that and then snags one of his soft pink lips between his vampiric teeth. The man who owns the motel has no time to come up with a story about pills or car accidents before Jude has him spread-eagle-hail-Mary on the office desk to discover an opening instead of a protrusion, the same opening the man who owns the motel will find on Jude two lifetimes from now.

Suffice it to say Jude stays at the motel free of cost for nearly three weeks.

And for nearly three weeks the man who owns

the motel watches from the window of the house, which he also owns. He watches the black cars pull in, swarming over black asphalt like slow-moving streams of black ants, and he watches the men who get out of those cars, sometimes the women. He remembers Jude doesn't have any money. And he goes into town for gas and groceries and he hears bad talk, and Jude's at the bowling alley, he's at the theater, he's out on the military base Serving Our Great Nation. What wicked intimacy. The man who owns the motel hears these things and he thinks he might like to kill one of those men who drive the black cars, kill him for the sin of getting what Jude gave him on the one and only night they spoke, for getting more. Oh god, it's inside of him, the image, it's inside of his head. Sometimes he thinks he can hear their voices on the wind, and he thinks he might like to come back to Jude with the severed head still dripping and say *SEE? SEE?* And there's an end to that thought that he can never get to, it's trapped in the loop. The man who owns the motel thinks this is the closest thing he's ever experienced to love and it feels like a cancer.

And then one night Jude takes home one of those good old American boys from the base, not in a black car this time but a Jeep the likes of which the man who owns the motel has only ever seen on the news. The wind carries the sound into his waiting green ear, first of loving, then of fighting, and then of a single gunshot without even a scream attached. He knows he should go down to the cabin but he doesn't, because maybe he runs into that good old American boy and maybe he has another bullet in the chamber or maybe he sees Jude. He's already done that song and dance and there's no question in his mind of which way it went just now. And he's tired, too; more tired than he was a second ago and so tired that he can in fact barely keep his eyes open. He falls asleep in his clothes and he wakes up on the first of the month.

So maybe third time's the charm, then, and this time it's so much more promising because he knows Jude. Not in real life, not how it counts, but from a men's room stall and a sailor bar advertisement with its head severed: FOR A GOOD TIME CALL JUDE. So tonight the man who owns the motel leaves the grounds and he goes to the sailor bar to play at people-things, with a plaid scarf around his mouth and a pair of socks shoved down the front of his corduroys. A man like him could choke on such wicked intimacy. He goes to the sailor bar and he goes into the men's room stall, he traces the marker-shape of the phone number that means Jude's still alive and then he takes a knee. He puts an eye to the hole he can't use the way he'd like to and he looks through it, into the other side, for posterity. And then he hears somebody's boots and makes a run for it and in that animal adrenaline he meets Jude.

His name is Jude and he likes boys, a lot, and the man who owns the motel isn't one of those and maybe he never was. But when they sit at the bar he remembers Jude doesn't have any money so he buys him a drink and later they're dancing. Setup and punchline. The man who owns the motel can't look at Jude's face and he can't listen to Jude's voice because he is remembering the way it had all looked and sounded a lifetime ago, when Jude got on his knees in the office and grazed those vampiric teeth against his inner thigh in what is now more dream than reality. He wonders if he's still a virgin and how this whole thing works, logistically speaking. This is the most thinking he will ever do on the subject.

Now Jude is pulling away, looking for somebody else's arms and looking back at him the whole time, teasing him, and it isn't fair, because Jude could have anybody he wants and the man who owns the motel has never had no one ever. The sailors look at Jude like they might want to swallow him up, and the man who owns the motel resents them for that. He doesn't think he wants to swallow Jude up, more so he wants to crawl inside of his ribcage and be dissolved in acid there like a fly in a pitcher plant. The man who owns the motel avoids their gazes on principle, fearing he could be swallowed up next, or that he could be laughed at. He avoids their gazes and watches Jude, tracing the white lightshapes he makes in the atmosphere. And then Jude winds up in the arms of John.

John is not a sailor and he is the man who, fifty years from now, will be rewarded with a podcast and a novel and a miniseries for turning Jude into a red Wikipedia link. He's clean-shaven and his eyes are black and Jude likes him, a lot. The man who owns the motel does not, but what does he know about wicked intimacy between two men? Jude calls him over and John buys drinks for the

PERFECT KISS STRICKOLL

both of them. When he laughs, it's the sound of a bird chewing on an electrical wire.

And then the man who owns the motel is following Jude out of the sailor bar, watching the halo of bleached frizz radiating from the back of his head under the streetlights, following him into the back of John's black car with John's four friends already inside. No more seats, only enough room to sit on strange laps, and isn't that so ha-ha funny for Jude? Not for the man who owns the motel, the man who cracks his protruding shoulders and prays to the God of mismatched socks in a pair. What a cold January night it is. They're going to the military base, or they're going out to the docks, and in the end it doesn't matter what the lie was because the truth is inland, no boats and no fish, not even a bay wind. The base becomes a speck on the horizon that Jude is too drunk and too self-satisfied to see.

The black car rolls to a stop next to the abandoned lot where tomorrow a skeleton will be found. The man who owns the motel is calm; he knows he's not going to die but unfortunately he can't say the same about Jude and he can't say he won't want to after whatever trainwreck this is starting to become. John rolls the car to a stop and he opens Jude's door and he pulls him onto the highway, his four friends following him. He pulls Jude into the abandoned lot. Jude does not yet know how bad things get, and the man who owns the motel thinks, unfairly, that Jude has never had his nose bloodied, his glasses broken, his long hair dragged into a motel room that locks. Least of all by his father.

The man who owns the motel presses his face into the black leather headrest in front of him and listens to the radio as the unspeakable act takes place.

When it's over John walks back to the car, hand in hand, with Jude. His four friends crawl off like drunken insects, their purpose served. Jude's naked from the waist down and he's not smiling anymore, and he's looking at the man who owns the motel with the pouting look that says he should have done something about this. Perhaps he should and perhaps he one day will—in that regard, he hopes Jude dies. John is saying something and laughing but the words are a fly. They're leaving now, Jude's sitting in his lap, not looking at him anymore. The man who owns the motel hates John for turning something he wanted into a stain, a shit, a great sucking black hole of pointless misery. This is to him a slight almost as great as the unspeakable act itself.

And where are they off to next? What potential lies in the slices John's headlights cleave into the pitch of the night, as he whistles the six-letter word for suicide to set his friends off in peals of vulture laughter? The man who owns the motel supposes it doesn't matter. But when the hot light of the NO VACANCY sign fries his eyes it also scoops out some not small portion of his guts.

What the man who owns the motel has failed to consider is that he is alive, that his stupid little life might register over the background hum of the universe. John comes to another stop and turns toward the backseat, on a neck joint that sounds rusted. He looks at the man who owns the motel for the first time. "Don't I know you?" he asks. "Don't I know you from somewhere?" It might even be true. The man who owns the motel wonders if John could have been one of those men who drove the black cars, the name that isn't quite so funny anymore, and that wonder brings two horrible thoughts to the forefront of his rotting mind: That it isn't such a clean cut from one to the other and that Jude might see between them too. Which means it's been a lot of shed blood for even more nothing.

But he's so tired, now, and thinks he doesn't want to be the man who owns the motel anymore. He doesn't want to be much of anything, much less master of the land where Jude dies. He gives John the key to the room he wants to drag Jude into by the hair and he lumbers back up to the house, and he draws the curtains shut, and he thinks, *I'll just sleep it off and start over tomorrow. I guess I mucked this one up pretty bad.*

But it takes six days for him to wake up on January first.

And he won't mess it up this time, he'll keep Jude with him, inside of him. In the office afterwards he holds Jude to his chest and he says the thing he couldn't say, that it had never happened before, that he wants it to happen again. He's finally learned what will make Jude bring a hand to the back of his head and curl cold pads of fingers against his scalp. And he takes Jude to the house, where he has never been, where he has never died. The man who owns the motel lays Jude down on the cotton sheets of the bed in his childhood room and Jude goes, of his own accord. He reaches up to take the glasses off the face of the man who owns the motel, blurring his vision out into bliss. His heart is pounding, pounding against the cage of his chest, beating, beating out—"I'm frightened," he says all at once, and it's true, he's scared. Has he spoken to Jude before? Of course; obviously; but not like this.

"I'm here," is all Jude says in return, hands in his hair, across the cheeks that have now grown wet with tears. "Look at me." The man who owns the motel doesn't need to be asked twice.

Jude, warm, hot, inside, Jude, wicked, inside, Jude, intimacy, Jude.

These and more than these, words out of order, thoughts untethered.

Afterwards they lie together on the cotton sheets of the bed in the childhood room of the man who owns the motel. They lie there for fifteen more years. Fifteen beautiful years where it doesn't rain a single day, where the green grass in the abandoned lot dries into a yellowed waste of space. The highway moves and it moves again and the money comes, sometimes in drips and drabs, sometimes in torrents. Jude's teeth wear down on smiles and the bones of good meat. The man who owns the motel smiles a lot these days, too, and when he hears whispers—Jude's at the bowling alley, he's at the theater, he's out on the military base that has now begun to distend with grotesque white maggot-napalm-bodies—he puts his fingers in his ears and smiles until his cheeks start to hurt. Now that he's got Jude it doesn't matter if he strays. Let him stray, thinks the man who owns the motel, so long as he comes back one way or another. Sometimes the fear returns and he thinks *my happiness is an intermission in some great show I never got the program for*, but sooner or later it goes away, usually once he's back in his childhood bed with Jude in his arms and his skin against Jude's skin. Fifteen years of this.

And then one hazy summer day in 1976 Jude goes out into the garage and he hangs himself, seemingly for no reason. No note, nothing. The man who owns the motel wakes up in a world with no war and no joint pain, no bald spot on the back of his head.

So on January first, 1960, he goes into town to the military store and he buys a gun, an awful metal animal of a thing and he lays it across his lap and he waits. Doesn't eat, doesn't sleep, doesn't get up even when the base of his spine starts to feel like somebody's hard at work driving a railroad spike between the vertebrae. Just waits. He waits for however Jude will come to him, battered and bleeding, shot, or maybe loving, the angel from the icebox. And he waits for what will follow behind Jude, salivating. If it comes down to that, thinks the man who owns the motel.

Come sunset the barrel of the gun is body-temperature and slick with clammy sweat from the palms of his hands. The man who owns the motel keeps waiting, his clothes stuck to his shivering body. He waits until the sun slips behind the military base and he waits until the dead light in the sky is as sickly and unsettled as he is and he sees the distant shape of Jude limping up the asphalt, the shape he now might recognize better than his own. He staggers to the left, and to the right, and then he clutches his stomach against the NO VACANCY sign and the man who owns the motel thinks *thank God, he's already shot.*

Then the man who owns the motel is running, running towards Jude now and he doesn't bother with the ambulance this time. He carries Jude into the backseat the way he might, in the stupid fantasy of the next world with new bodies, carry him to their marriage bed. His blood beads across the lacquered upholstery in discrete drops that might look perverse if the man who owns the motel could look at anything or in fact even think of perversion. No perversion tonight; Jude's already shot.

It's off to the hospital, then, the hospital on the base, it's the emergency room, the emergency surgery. "If you brought him in even a second later," it's the nurse saying, her red lipstick matching Jude's bloody smear across his own mouth, "we'd have been taking him out of here in a body bag." She might have said that, if she really existed; her voice sounded awfully like that of the man who owns the motel. But he's so hoarse now from shouting that he thinks he might never say anything again.

It's looking at Jude now, somewhere sterile, somewhere cleaner than he could ever be. Was he

PERFECT KISS STRICKOLL

really quite so small, so crumpled into himself? The bed swallows him. And the monitor that says he's alive is beeping, and beeping, and failing to beep, and beeping.

The clock is ticking along, seconds melting into nothing, eleven fifty, eleven fifty-one. The man who owns the motel gets out of his plastic chair, the one he stole with the wife-lie. That hurt him but it was worth it, somewhere—bitter ends for the world's means. He kneels on the sterile tile floor and he does something he has not done since he was thirteen years old; he says a prayer.

"Please," he says, scratches from the back of his ruined throat, and he means to say something else but everything else, even *Jude*, burns too much. "Please."

And he looks back up at the clock as it ticks towards eleven fifty-two.

"Please."

Eleven fifty-three.

Please . . .

Please . . .

Please . . .

Please . . .

Please . . .

How does Libro.fm work?

Libro.fm makes it possible for you to buy audiobooks through our bookstore. But how?

1 Profits from your monthly membership and à la carte audiobook purchases are shared with our bookstore.

2 Libro.fm requires no extra work and no money on the bookstore's end. Why? Because they want more money in local communities, where it can make the greatest impact.

3 When you sign up to support our bookstore with a Libro.fm membership, you provide us with sustained, reliable income over time, so we can stay serving the community—and keeping the lights on.

4 And you'll enjoy curated playlists and recommendations from expert booksellers like us, along with a simple and thoughtful listening platform.

https://libro.fm/indie-partners/resources?bookstore=ghoulishbookstore

ABOUT OUR GHOULS

Saswati Chatterjee currently resides in New Delhi, India. A lifelong fan of horror, video games, and dragons, she's also got a bit of a soft corner for the occasional artificial intelligence. She can usually be found at her Twitter, yelling bad opinions about TV shows.

Jen Conley is the author of the Anthony Award winning YA novel, *Seven Ways to Get Rid of Harry* and the Anthony Award nominated short story collection, *Cannibals: Stories from the Edge of the Pine Barrens*. She lives in Brick, New Jersey.

Lor Gislason is a writer and occasional editor from Vancouver Island, Canada. Ask them about their current hyperfixation or their cat Pierogi Platter and they'll love you forever.

Lena Ng shambles around Toronto, Canada, and is a zombie member of the Horror Writers Association. She has curiosities published in weighty tomes including *Amazing Stories* and Flame Tree's *Asian Ghost Stories* and *Weird Horror Stories*. *Under an Autumn Moon* is her short story collection.

Jess Hagemann's recent work has appeared in *Sky Island Journal*, *Castle of Horror: Young Adult*, and *Into the Forest: Tales of the Baba Yaga*. She has an MFA from the Jack Kerouac School. Her debut novel *Headcheese* won an IPPY Award in Horror. www.jesshagemann.com

Justin Lutz is the Splatterpunk Award nominated author of *Gemini Rising, ACAB Includes Animal Control,* and the short story collection *Gone to Seed*. He lives on the river in Pennsylvania with his wife and cats and believes in Bigfoot, strong coffee, and the healing power of Bruce Springsteen.

Shannon Riley is a writer and therapist from Pennsylvania who, as a teen, wrote gore starring her friends and family instead of doing math homework. Now she writes because there's truth in fiction, and little truth anywhere else. She's written for the *Dark Blooms* anthology, and her first book, *Pocketknife Kitty*, debuts June 2024. Twitter: @shannon_said

E.F. Schraeder believes in ghosts, magic, and dogs. Schraeder is the author of *The Price of a Small Hot Fire* (Raw Dog Screaming Press, 2023), *What Happened Was Impossible* (Ghoulish Books, 2023), the Imadjinn Award finalist *Liar: Memoir of a Haunting* (Omnium Gatherum, 2021), and other works.

Danger Slater is the Wonderland-Award winning author of *I Will Rot Without You, Moonfellows, He Digs a Hole,* and other books too. He has a mustache. Or maybe he shaved it by now. Or maybe he is already dead. I don't know when you're reading this.

Live Spooky, Die Spooky.

perfect kiss strickoll (he/she) is a writer and film student currently located in sunny California. He likes to write about sad queers with bizarre interpersonal hang-ups, as informed by his lifelong love and study of the horror genre. She and her other publications can be found on Twitter @pkstrickoll.

Jennifer Elise Wang (she/they) is a nonbinary femme in STEM and punk rock pretty boi poet from Dallas, Texas, U.S.A. When she's not in lab or writing, she enjoys action sports, aerials, burlesque, and rescuing cats. They have been published in *FERAL, Exist Otherwise, Open Minds Quarterly*, and *Darling Lit*.

Stephanie M. Wytovich is an American poet, novelist, and essayist. She is a recipient of the Elizabeth Matchett Stover Memorial Award, the Bram Stoker Award, the Ladies of Horror Fiction Writers Grant, and has received the Rocky Wood Memorial Scholarship for non-fiction writing. Keep up with her writing at https://stephaniemwytovich.substack.com/.

DO YOU WANT TO WRITE FOR GHOULISH TALES?

We will reopen for Ghoulish Tales Issue #3 on February 1st and close on March 29th, 2024. Writers are encouraged to submit their best stories to ghoulishsubmissions@gmail.com with [TITLE] – [LAST NAME] – [STORY/ESSAY] in the subject line. Please do not copy/paste the story in the body of the email. We prefer Word doc attachments if possible. All inquiries can also be directed to the same address. Stories received after March 29th will be deleted unread. For an idea of what we are looking to publish, please refer to the stories in the issue you are currently holding in your hands.

Word count: 5,000 max (short stories) 2,000 max (non-fiction); Payment: 10c per word; Simultaneous Submissions: Yes; Multiple Submissions: No; Reprints: No.

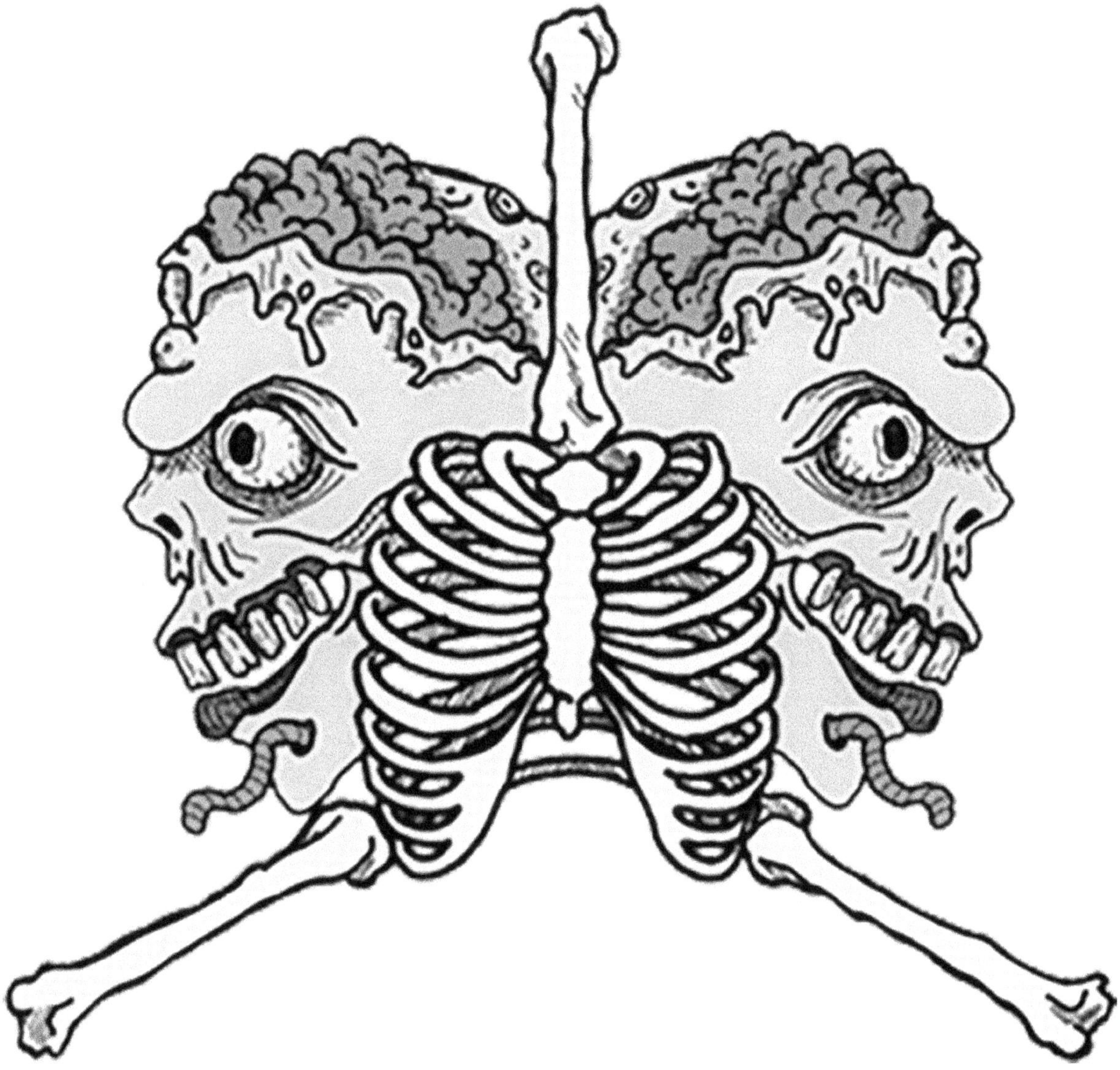